T0274437

DISCOVER

A Calypso's Journey Novel

www.mascotbooks.com

DISCOVER: A Calypso's Journey Novel

For more information, please contact:
Mascot Books, an imprint of Amplify Publishing Group
620 Herndon Parkway, Suite 220
Herndon, VA 20170
info@amplifypublishing.com

Cover illustration by Maggie Donaghy

Library of Congress Control Number: 2023910297
CPSIA Code: PRV1023A
ISBN-13: 978-1-63755-852-2
Printed in the United States

To anyone out there who feels a little alone.
Because we all know book characters, no matter
how fictional they are, can be the greatest friends.

DISCOVER

A Calypso's Journey Novel

ISABELLA GERBORG

CONTENTS

CHAPTER 1
MORE THAN FRIENDS

"Turn up the volume!"

Spencer takes his hand off the steering wheel. The cart begins to rattle as the bass booms more intensely, releasing a fizz of serotonin throughout my body. We are currently blasting "Fancy" by Iggy Azalea as we zoom down the road on his golf cart. My best friend, Sadie, laughs at a joke he makes. The music is so loud I can barely hear what anyone is saying. Exhilaration rushes through me. The warm breeze brushing against my face gives me a sense of freedom. This is why I love summer.

"Who thinks I could jump off right now and do a backflip midair?" Trevor asks, looking at me.

"I think you're overestimating your abilities."

"Overestimating? What are you talking about?"

"C'mon, Trev," Spencer says. "I don't need anyone getting hurt while I'm in the driver's seat."

"You only live once."

"Oh yeah, Spencer. Let this kid do something dangerous. It'll help him live longer," Sadie says sarcastically.

"Trevor, were you able to find someone to take you home?" I ask.

"Oh, yeah, I'll be fine. I'm staying with Spencer."

"Oh okay."

Part of me wants the conversation to continue, but there's nothing else to talk about. I flip my attention back to the front of the cart.

"Your neighborhood is gorgeous," Sadie says as we turn left on Norman Street and on our way to Spencer's house.

"You've been here before."

"I know. But the jealousy kicks in every time."

"Why? 'Cause my parents are rich brats? That doesn't have anything to do with me."

Spencer may be part of a rich family, but he hates being associated with them. He has made that very clear to us. His Korean dad is the CEO of some paperwork company, and his New Yorker mom is a surgeon at the hospital here in Brevard, North Carolina. I haven't had many interactions with them, but from what I know, his mom is all business and his dad is that plus abusive.

Spencer, on the other hand, has a more edgy style. He frequently wears eyeliner and has a very dark punk style with three different tattoos. He's a year ahead of us in school but was also held back, making him sixteen. His older sister, Kelsea, took him to the tattoo parlor as soon as his sixteenth birthday hit. Their dad was furious as soon as he found out.

"Did y'all see Carla before we left?" I ask, starting a new topic.

"Oh, how she wanted to come with us?" Sadie says. "Yeah, that was weird."

"What did she call her imaginary friend again?" Trevor asks.

"I think it was Hayley or something."

"Yeah, some days I'd just be walking down the hall and catch Carla talking to air,"

Trevor says. "God, she freaks me out."

"Guys, come on," Spencer interrupts.

"What?" I question his tone.

"Y'all are going into high school now."

"Yeah, so?"

"So you need to stop wasting your time over this immature Carla girl. You're better than that."

"Okay, true," Sadie says, quieting down.

"I guess you're right. And if we wanna get more friends in high school, it would be better if we invited her to something. We don't want anyone on our bad side." Trevor laughs. "Weren't you the one just saying how annoying she is?"

I ignore him. "Oh, Sadie, I talked to Teresa the other day. You know, my friend from art class? Yeah, so since we'll all be in school together next year, I figured you two have to meet. She's so nice. You'll love her. I already set up a coffee date for the three of us on Tuesday."

"What? But my brother has—"

"Why are you always so worried about your brother? He needs to learn to take care of himself."

"But . . . okay, fine. I guess he can ride with Liam again."

Liam is Spencer's younger brother. Every Tuesday and Friday, Liam and Sadie's brother, Drew, have soccer practice. Sometimes they'll carpool together, but I know Sadie prefers to take him to practice herself. She likes the extra quality time they get while bike riding. She can be a bit overprotective of him, but I see where she is coming from.

We all grow silent. The song has now changed to "Dark Horse" by Katy Perry. I know this isn't Spencer's type of music. He made a playlist with all of Sadie's favorite songs, which happen to include some of the latest pop music. He listens to it whenever he wants to think about her. It puts him in a better mood.

"So . . . y'all are gonna join Spencer and I on Sunday?"

"Hell yeah!" Trevor exclaims. "Last time was a blast!"

"I still don't understand this whole double dating thing. Me and Trevor are just friends."

Sadie throws me a look as Trevor asks, "Where are we at this time?"

"Ummm . . ."

"The Square Root," Spencer decides. "Five o' clock."

"Oh my god, yes! I love that place. So, Cal, what do you say?"

"Fine," I grumble, a little overdramatically. "I guess I'll go."

As I gaze at Trevor's lovely maroon hair, I know that we are more than friends.

CHAPTER 2
HARD DECISIONS

"I just wish Violet would be nicer to me," I vent to Sadie. "I know your mom is annoying, but at least you have your brother. My mom still treats me like I'm five, and my dad and sister rarely acknowledge my presence."

"You act like my life is so perfect. My mom is always off drinking, and if we ever have a conversation, she doesn't even remember it the next day. I try to talk to her about how much it hurts me and how I have to take care of my brother all the time, but she just yells at me, saying I don't appreciate all she's done for us. My dad has done more for us, and he's not even living here."

"Why don't you just go live with your dad?"

"Well . . . then I would be away from you."

"That's true. Forget what I said. I never want you to move away again."

Sadie doesn't reply. Does she not agree with me? Does she want to move back to Nashville? She already lived there with her dad in first and second grade. I hated it. For those two years, I lost my best friend. I was overwhelmed with excitement when I got the news Sadie was coming back. Then when we became next-door neighbors, I grew even more ecstatic. But Sadie still isn't responding to my comment, and it's worrying me. Realizing I'm biting the inside of my cheek a little too hard, I try to ease my nerves.

"Did you hear what I said?"

"Yeah, sorry. I was just thinking."

We continue walking beside each other in silence. I stare down at my white Converse shoes. Sadie is quite a reserved person, but we have known each other for so long. I know almost everything about her. When we were in kindergarten, her parents got divorced. That was really hard for Sadie, especially since her mom was six months pregnant with her brother at the time. Sadie's relationship with her mom has always been complicated. That's why she moved to Nashville with her dad. But since the end of second grade, she has stayed in Brevard.

I glance at Sadie now, wondering what she is thinking. Her light brown hair reaches her collarbone. She looks down at her dirty white tennis shoes touching the sidewalk and heaves a sigh as we approach our houses, hers noticeably smaller than mine.

"See you tomorrow!" I cheer as Sadie walks through her front yard.

"See you tomorrow," she echoes.

I stroll up my long, flat driveway and over to the front porch. I pass the wooden swing to my left and head to the front door. I jiggle the key into the doorknob and step inside. The white "G" sign hits the door lightly as I slam it shut. The "G" stands for Gresham, my family's last name.

The flooring in our house is dark cherrywood, and the walls of the front room are white. The dining room is to my right when I walk in. I glance at the useless coat rack in front of it, wondering why we still own that thing. To the left is a storage closet. I take off my shoes and set them by the front door before walking ahead, past the stairs, and entering the kitchen. To the right of the kitchen is the bathroom and a door to the garage. To the left of the kitchen is the living room. The back door stands between these two areas.

When I was born, my biological parents didn't want a child, so I was taken to an adoption center in Waynesville. That's where my new parents found me at four years old. Part of me wishes I remembered more of my childhood before I lived here, but part of me doesn't care.

My parents are sitting in two of the barstools eating a salad my mom made. She is always on some kind of diet or weight-loss program, which I don't understand because her body already fits into all of society's beauty standards. But I don't care that much.

She can do whatever makes her happy, as long as it doesn't affect me.

My dad is tall and big. He works for a financial business, and my mom is a fashion designer. I don't know much about their jobs, except that they somehow make enough money to afford this house and expensive cars. My dad isn't as odd as my mom, but he doesn't talk to me much. I always wonder why they adopted me in the first place. They seem very satisfied with their biological child, Violet. My mom acts like she cares about me, but I know it's all one large performance.

"Hey, Calypso!" my mom says, squealing in her high-pitched baby voice as I enter the room. "How were Sadie and the others?"

"They were good. Here's the key."

I set the rusty brass key on the counter and walk over to the fridge.

"Would you like to sit with us? I made a salad with walnuts, carrots, zucchini, and cucumbers."

"No, I'm good." Instead, I grab a Coke and a slice of cold pizza and head for the stairs.

"But, sweetie, I care for you, and if you don't eat these veggies, then you won't grow up into a healthy adult."

"Mom, just stop. I'm about to be in high school. I can eat whatever I want."

"Someone's gained some sass," Dad mumbles as I stomp up the stairs. "Where's Violet?"

"Off at a friend's house. Do you need something from her?" Mom asks.

"No, I was just wondering."

As I'm walking down the hall, I notice a salty taste in my mouth. Blood. This happens to me all the time. More often than not, I don't realize I'm doing it. It's like one of those bad habits that you subconsciously repeat over and over until it becomes uncontrollable. My subconscious habit is biting my cheek when I'm nervous.

I open the door to my room and walk over to the nightstand. After taking a couple cool sips of water, the salty taste disappears. My bedroom is the only thing I love about this house. It's me in a nutshell. The walls are dark maroon. My queen-size bed has a comfortable olive green bedspread laying on top of it. I have my own bathroom to the left of my bed. The door to my closet is next to that. All the hardwood furniture is black. I walk over to my dresser and glance out the window to my right. I catch a small peek of the backyard before returning my eyes back to the pile of clothes on top of my dresser.

I change into pajamas, hop onto my bed, and fetch a piece of paper with my favorite pencil. It has Bob Ross on it. Munching on a slice of cold pepperoni pizza, I recall what Ms. Franscene told me last week. Let your pencil do the work. Ms. Franscene owns an art studio called Happy Little Accidents. I've been going there for almost a year now. It's where I met Teresa. Teresa and I are both Ms. Franscene's favorite students.

She wants us to become interns when we turn sixteen. The studio is not very popular. No more than ten other kids show up to classes, and Ms. Franscene and her wife are the only teachers. But it's still my favorite place to be. Ms. Franscene is one of the sweetest people I know, and Teresa is my closest friend besides Sadie.

As I continue to draw, thoughts of Trevor block my brain. Part of me wants to tell him that I like him, but the other part of me is too scared he only considers me a friend. Maybe I should keep it that way. Another part of me isn't even completely sure I like Trevor. Maybe it's just my hormones acting up. I hate not knowing what the right thing to do is. I just wish there would be someone who could make all the hard decisions for me. That way, nothing would ever be my fault.

CHAPTER 3
IT'S COMPLICATED

Happy Fourth of July. Tonight we are hosting a barbecue with friends in our backyard. Sadie's family, Spencer's family, Trevor, and Teresa are going to be here, as well as Carla's family.

I introduced Sadie to Teresa a few days after school ended. I assumed it would be difficult for the two to be friends. Since Sadie is more reserved and pessimistic, I thought she would take Teresa's kindness as overwhelming and fake. But the moment the two of them sparked conversation, I knew they'd get along perfectly. Tonight will be Teresa's first time meeting Trevor and Spencer. When I sent a picture of Spencer, Teresa said she thinks he was in her lit class last year. The two of them are going into sophomore year. Even though Teresa hasn't met the guys yet, I already feel like she's a part of our friend group. Carla tagged along with Sadie, Trevor, and me once since the last day of school. She's nice and friendly, but still not my favorite person to be around.

I'm currently setting up for later while my parents are working in their office. I was expecting Mom to be frantic, making sure I don't burn myself while flipping the burgers. But I guess her fashion work is more important right now. I adjust the volume on my earbuds, classical music humming through my eardrums. Other than indie and pop, classical is one of my favorite genres. Instead of the distracting words, I can actually pay attention to the raw notes and sound. I also enjoy making up stories in my head to go along with the music.

I notice the silver whoosh of Violet's car in my peripheral vision. I don't care where or why she is leaving. She's probably off to Brittany's or on her way to "hang out" with George, her boyfriend. I've never officially met him, now that I think about it. He's been at our house several times. My parents adore him as if he's their own son. The times he's been over, I stay put in my room and the entire family forgets about me. My mom never asks, "Why didn't you come down to see George?" They don't care. I bet they rather me not be there in the first place.

∽

Time flies, and soon, I'm gathered around the firepit with my friends.

"And look who's wearing platforms today," Sadie teases me. "Trying to make yourself look taller?"

"Oh, come on. The doctor said I could still grow an inch or two!"

"Bullshit. I'll always be taller than you."

"Whatever."

"Y'all have such a noticeable height difference," Spencer comments, the raspiness of his voice coming through.

"And I'm even taller," Teresa says.

"Why is everyone attacking me?"

"We're not attacking you," Sadie says. "It's just a joke."

"Maybe it's good to be short. I was always made fun of for being the tall, fat kid that sounds like a boy."

Teresa laughs after making that remark, but by the sadness in her soft brown eyes, I can tell that it truly hurts. I never know what to say when she bullies herself, but I try my best to be as supportive as I can. She tucks her wavy brown hair with blonde highlights behind her ear, another sign she feels awkward.

"Forget about those bullies," I say. "I think you look beautiful."

"Yeah, sometimes people say shitty things just to make you feel stupid about yourself," Spencer adds.

Trevor is talking less than usual, but I don't waste time questioning it. He has his occasional quiet moods. He's probably just thinking about his complicated home life. His mother got sick from lung cancer and passed away when he was only seven years old. His father is too busy to acknowledge his kids' existence. When he does talk to Trevor, it always turns into an argument. The only other person Trevor could turn to is his older sister, but she is going into her sophomore year of college and spends most of her time away from home.

Trevor only opened up to me about this a few months ago. When he did, he broke into tears, then felt super embarrassed. I don't think he's ever going to talk about it again. I wish I could hug him right now and tell him everything is going to be okay. I wish he knew how much I thought about him. But I don't even know how he feels about me.

When I return my focus back to the conversation, I hear Carla blurt out, "That reminds me of the time I peed my pants in class."

Sadie, Spencer, Trevor, and I exchange a look. The secondhand embarrassment is really kicking in. I don't even know how we got here.

"Oh sorry. Did I confuse y'all? I meant to say when I was in kindergarten."

"Oh okay," I say, adding a laugh that is obviously fake. "But what does that have to do with anything we were saying?"

She shrugs, that innocent, childlike smile still plastered on her face. "Just reminded me of it."

Carla's mom, Mrs. Robinson, walks over. She's young, maybe in her midthirties, and greatly resembles Carla. The only difference is her eyes are green and Carla's are bright blue. Carla must have her father's eyes.

"How's the party going over here?"

"Good," we all reply in unison.

"I'm glad! Carla's not been invited to too many parties before."

"Yeah, well, we're glad she's here," I say, partially lying. Again, there's nothing wrong with Carla. She just makes me uncomfortable at times.

Carla's dark brown hair is tied up into space buns, which I'm beginning to notice is her signature look. Her wispy bangs add to her youthful nature.

She has a small button nose and a bit of a baby-like face. She went all out in Fourth of July swag—red skinny jeans; a tie-dyed red, white, and blue T-shirt; and light-up American flag glasses.

When Sadie heads inside to go to the bathroom, I zone out of the current conversation and gaze at the scene of the night. Drew and Liam are playing soccer in the back corner of the yard. All the adults are sitting around the front porch table, except for Mr. and Mrs. Robinson, who are hovering closer to the driveway.

Sadie's mom is definitely drunk. She is holding a large can of beer while staggering around the porch laughing. The rest of the adults don't seem to be too concerned. They are talking and chuckling with her. Her loud voice booms a comment I can't understand due to the thick slurring of her words. Suddenly, she lifts the cup to her mouth but misses, spilling Bud Light on her blue T-shirt. The adults gasp and laugh. I watch Sadie's mom attempting to clean up her mess but doing a terrible job. My parents head inside to grab a towel for Ms. Adams. Adams is her maiden name. Sadie and Drew still have their dad's last name, Lovington.

Ms. Adams has been suffering from an alcohol addiction for a long time. Sadie kept her secret from me until seventh grade, but even after that, she doesn't talk about it much. Sometimes I wish she shared more of her feelings with me. It's as if she doesn't trust me. Aren't best friends supposed to trust each other with everything?

Everyone leaves around 9:30 p.m., other than Trevor and Teresa. The mood has died down. I'm not sure where my parents have gone off to. They must be inside the house, cleaning up. Trevor, Teresa, and I are staring at our phones in silence. Finally, a red Toyota pulls up.

"Oh, that's my sister," Trevor says. "It was nice hanging out with y'all."

"Yeah, it was fun," Teresa adds.

"It was."

When Trevor gets to me, we awkwardly stand there for a minute. My lips begin to tingle as I think of kissing him, and my stomach clenches with butterflies. But ew, no.

He's just my friend. We come together for an uncomfortable half hug, and I watch as he treks down the driveway.

"Bye, Trevor!" I shout, my teeth letting go of my right cheek.

"Bye, Cal! I had so much fun tonight!"

"Me too!"

He waves me goodbye one last time before he closes the door to the passenger seat and his face disappears into the night.

"You totally have a crush on him," Teresa says. "It's so obvious."

"Is it really that bad?"

"Oh my god, I knew it!"

"I mean, I don't know. It's so complicated. What if he doesn't feel the same about me? Right now we're great friends, and I don't wanna ruin that."

"That makes sense. I'm here to talk about it anytime, you know."

I decide to change the conversation and put the spotlight on her. I don't like talking about things I'm unsure about.

"So how are things with Josh?" I ask.

"Oh. Actually . . . we broke up like a month ago."

"What? No way. Why didn't you tell me?"

"I don't know. It just never came up."

"What happened?"

"Well, I . . . I don't know. It's hard to explain. We didn't agree on a lot of things and he was starting to turn into kind of an asshole. I just don't think he's my type anymore."

"Yeah, that makes sense. I think you did the right thing, then."

She peers down at her phone, looking for a text from her mom, but sighs, seeing no new responses. She puts her phone away and looks at the ground for a minute.

"Actually, there's more. It wasn't just random things we didn't agree on. He was homophobic. Like really disgustingly homophobic. And I figured out . . . I'm bisexual."

"Wait, really?"

"Yeah."

"Oh, wow! How are you feeling about it?"

I'm not exactly sure how I'm supposed to react. I want to show my support without accidentally offending her.

"I mean . . . more like myself than I have in years."

"That's so great! I'm so happy for you!"

"Thank you."

"I'm always here to support you."

"Me too."

"Have you told anyone else?"

"Only Ms. Franscene. I'm too scared to post about it because I don't know what anyone else would say, and I can't tell my family. My parents already favor my brothers, and they would hate me even more if they knew."

"That sucks. But I'm glad you told me. And if you ever wanna talk more about it, I'm here."

She embraces me in a tight hug and trembles. "I'm really scared."

"It's okay. It's gonna be okay. You're so brave."

"I know, but I'm serious. If my parents ever find out, I'm doomed."

"I'm so sorry. I wish it didn't have to be like this."

"Me too," she says, her voice breaking up. She lets go of me and sniffles. "Oh, speaking of the devil," she mutters as her mom's car appears.

We say our goodbyes, and I stand there for a minute, the rush of the night beginning to fade into exhaustion. I head back inside the house, Teresa's tight hug and trembling fear still heavy on my mind. It's sad she has to feel so afraid of being herself.

But all I can do is keep being the comforting friend she needs.

CHAPTER 4
THE OTHER GIRL

Today is the first day of high school. I'm sitting in the back of Violet's car right now, the nerves of anxiety mixed with excitement taking over me. Sadie is to my left, gazing out the window at the parking lot. In just a few minutes, I'll be walking through those black double doors. With high school comes new beginnings and new friendships.

I can't wait to see where life takes me.

I start thinking about Sadie sleeping over at my house last night. We had a fun time, but the energy didn't feel right. I think there might be something going on with Sadie's family, but I don't want to make her uncomfortable by asking. I tried to cheer her up by putting on *Mean Girls* and making unicorn popcorn, a favorite childhood snack of ours. But she fell asleep early while I watched the entire movie alone. This morning Sadie apologized for sleeping during the movie, and she seemed to be doing better, so hopefully everything is fine.

Sadie and I get out of the car and wander toward the school. We have most of our classes together, except third, fourth, and sixth period. Carla is in my seventh-period class, algebra. I don't have any classes with Trevor, which is sad, but at least we'll see each other during lunch. According to Teresa, the school allows most of the freshmen to have the same lunch period.

We're walking down the hall, looking for my first class, when I feel a tap on my shoulder. I whip around to see Trevor. I haven't seen him since the barbecue last month. I've been too scared to talk to him now that I've realized I think of him as more than a friend. I'm scared because I don't know how he feels or how he'd react if I told him. Teresa says I'm taking this way too seriously and that I need to calm down. She thinks I should still text him so he doesn't think I'm being avoidant. I just don't know. Your feelings can play tricks on you like that sometimes.

"Hey, what's up?" I say, trying to act casual, but I cringe at the way my voice went really high-pitched on "up." Why am I so awkward?

"Any reason you've been ignoring me for the past month?"

Shit. I guess I should've listened to Teresa. This whole situation just went from awkward to unbearable.

"Oh my god, no! I'd never ignore you, or I—at least I never wanted to ignore you. I just, you see, I've been so busy, and I kept meaning to text. I just . . . I'm sorry."

"I see," he replies with a slight grin. "No need to apologize. You just kinda left me hangin', you know?"

"Yeah, I know."

We laugh for a second, then he asks, "Did Sadie come with you?"

I'm about to say "yes" and point to her next to me, but she's nowhere to be found. She was here a minute ago. Maybe I was too tired to notice, but where could she have gone without telling me?

"I don't know. She was here a second ago." I'm completely freaking out.

"Calm down, calm down. I'm sure she's fine."

He may be right, but something doesn't feel normal. She's been acting weird ever since last night. Maybe I'm the problem. But why would she hate me? What did I do wrong?

"I guess," I mumble, even though I'm still uptight.

"What's your first class again?"

"Lit."

"Ugh, mine's bio. It freaking sucks we don't have any classes together."

"I know," I say, self-conscious of how gross my voice sounds. "But, um . . . I'll see you at lunch."

"Wait!" Trevor exclaims before I continue down the hall. The ten-minute warning bell rings right on cue. Swarms of students scurry around us. I notice some other freshmen wearing confused and flustered faces as they try to find their classes.

"What is it?"

"I'm . . . um, you know, I'm free . . . tonight. If you wanted to hang out or something, that would be cool. What about a movie?"

I'm speechless and probably wearing the oddest expression on my face, but this really jolts me awake. What should I say? What kind of smile do I make? I thought I would be the one making the first move, but here he comes out of the blue.

"There's the new *Guardians of the Galaxy* movie," he suggests. "What about that?"

I don't tell him I've already seen it. Instead, I awkwardly exclaim, "Yes, that's perfect! Can't wait!"

He winks at me, catching me even more off guard. I giggle in response as the butterflies worsen. I feel like I'm going to throw up. I can't believe what has just happened. Not only is today the first day of high school, but it's also the day of my first date. This cannot be real.

I turn the corner and head to my class. When I enter the room, I spot Sadie sitting in the back corner. I notice an empty spot next to her and mentally claim that as mine.

When I sit down, I ask, "Where did you go?"

"I don't know. You were talking to Trevor, so I thought I didn't need to be there anymore."

"What? Who said you couldn't stay with us? It's better than me freaking out trying to find you. You at least could've told me where you were going."

"I just didn't feel like it, okay?"

"Okay."

This is not how I expected the first day to go, and I still have six more periods after this. I have no idea what's coming.

The lunch bell rings. I rush through the halls, cutting in front of the slow walkers, on my way to the cafeteria. I pull out my phone and text Sadie.

Lets meet in the cafeteria :)

I haven't seen Sadie since second period, and because she was acting moody this morning, I wasn't able to tell her about my date with Trevor. Butterflies are still buzzing through me as I picture the two of us sitting side by side in the movie chairs tonight, staring up at the screen, bonding over a bucket of popcorn. I can't believe this is actually happening. I've known him since third grade, and now we're actually going on a date.

When I reach the cafeteria, I see Teresa in the first lunch line. I scurry over to her and begin to ramble about Trevor.

"Oh my god, guess what? Trevor asked me out on a date! We're going to see a movie!"

"Wait, for real? When?" Teresa asks.

"Tonight."

"What movie?"

"*Guardians of the Galaxy.*"

"Oh yes, that movie is so good!" she exclaims. "Wait, so did you tell him? That you like him?"

"No, I didn't even have to say anything. He just asked. And he was sad about me not texting him and—"

"Wait, stop. Here he comes now."

"Hey, guys," Trevor says from behind me. "Where are we gonna sit?"

"I don't know. Somewhere in here, I guess," I say, trying to sound chill.

"Wait, so do we all have the same lunch?" Teresa asks.

"I think so. I see Carla over there. I guess we should ask if she wants to sit with us. I don't know where Sadie is, though. I texted her earlier. Normally, she texts back fast, but I don't know. She's being weird today."

"I'm sure it's fine," Teresa comforts. "She might just be having a hard time adjusting to high school."

"I don't know," I sulk. I miss Sadie's enthusiasm. I want to know what's going on, but I don't want to start any drama. I know she can be sensitive at times.

"I wouldn't worry about it, Cal," Trevor says. "You're probably just overthinking it. Maybe she left class late or got lost."

"Got lost? How?"

"You know what I'm saying." He smirks, his left dimple revealing itself. No, I actually don't know what he's saying, but I don't bother asking. "I'm gonna go sit down."

"Okay," we reply.

Teresa and I each grab a tray with three bland chicken tenders and a sad roll of bread. We head over to the table Trevor saved for us. Carla and Spencer joined him while we were getting our food. As I'm walking over, I notice Sadie rushing into the cafeteria, her face flushed red with what looks like shame. Or is it fear? I can't tell.

Teresa sits down, but I stay standing so I can talk to Sadie.

"Hey, is everything okay? I texted you, but—"

"Everything's fine. Sorry, I meant to reply. I was just . . . busy."

"Busy?" I scoff. "What the hell is that supposed to mean?"

She lowers her voice and mumbles, "I really don't wanna talk about this right now. Okay? I'm so sorry. This doesn't have anything to do with you. I promise."

"What? Now I'm scared."

"You don't need to be scared. Everything's fine."

"Okay, but if something is wrong, you know you can tell me, right?"

"Yeah, I know."

"Hey, Sadie, you good?" Spencer asks as we both take a seat.

She nods. I offer her one of my chicken fingers since she doesn't have any food for herself. She smiles and takes it. Trevor and Spencer are cracking jokes about some girl in their class who is trying to flirt with Spencer even though she knows he's dating Sadie. I can't focus on what anyone is saying. I'm too zoned out in my own thoughts. Something is bothering Sadie, but she doesn't want to tell me. What is it, and why does it need to be kept secret?

A few minutes before lunch ends, Teresa and I head to the bathroom. The middle stall is occupied, so we take the other two. I use the big one at the end.

I hear Teresa's toilet and the other girl's flush before mine and listen as they both walk out of their stalls.

"I love your outfit," Teresa says.

"Thank you! I'm really diggin' yours too."

"Aw, thanks! I don't think we've met before. Are you a freshman?"

"No, I'm a sophomore. My family and I moved here over the summer for my mom's job, so that could be why you haven't seen me before."

"What great jobs are there in Brevard?" Teresa asks.

I exit my stall and head over to the sinks to find Teresa and the other girl standing to the right. Her long dark hair is styled in intricate dreads. She's between my height and Teresa's. Her deep brown eyes shine against the light from the ceiling and her smile is big and vibrant. She's dressed in a black T-shirt and olive green pants that are held up by a rainbow belt. Her wrist must be weighted down by the amount of bracelets she's wearing. What ties the whole outfit together are the classy black headphones around her neck.

Just as I thought the conversation was coming to an end, Teresa's new friend adds, "So you a sophomore too?"

"Yeah."

"Ah, let's go!"

Teresa laughs, and the other girl continues. Wow, she sure is chatty.

"You have any siblings that go here?"

"No, I have two brothers, but they're both younger. One's in third grade, and the other is in first."

"Oh. I have an older brother. He's a senior. We're besties."

Teresa laughs shortly. "My brothers are brats."

"Younger siblings do tend to be troublemakers."

"Yeah."

"You should come sit with me and Kyle—my brother," the girl suggests. "That would be so fun. But lemme tell you, him and his friends get a little crazy at times."

"Well, um, that sounds . . . I don't know. My friend right here has to tell me something kinda important, so . . . you know . . ."

"Oh well, maybe another day then."

"Yeah. Another day."

"Did I ever catch your name?" the new girl asks right as her hand reaches for the door.

"Teresa."

"That's so pretty! I'm Nala. After the lion in *Lion King*. My mom is obsessed with '90s Disney movies."

"Oh, wow, I love that! See you around, Nala."

"See you around."

I turn to Teresa with a mischievous smile on my face.

"Stop it." Teresa grins, her light brown cheeks turning rosy pink.

"Oh, c'mon! She even invited you to sit with her."

"I don't know. She could've just been being nice. She seemed very social."

"But she was interested in you. Even I could tell. She kept the conversation going and everything. And weren't you interested in her?"

"It's never gonna happen. She's way too cool for me. And we don't even know anything about her."

"You're just doubting yourself. And it's obvious. Your face is so red right now."

"Oh god, it is?" she shrieks, her hands touching her face as she looks in the mirror, attempting to cover it up. "Ew, that's so embarrassing." I laugh as Teresa continues, "Okay, I have to admit, she was pretty attractive. But there's no way she'd ever like someone like me."

"What do you mean someone like you? You're gorgeous!"

Teresa gives me a look of hesitancy. "Still . . ."

"Fine," I determine. "I'll help you."

CHAPTER 5
FIRST DATE

arrive home from school to find my mom cleaning in the kitchen and my dad on the couch watching golf with a bag of Lay's.

"Hey, so, uh . . . guys," I stutter uncomfortably. "I have to tell you something."

"Sure. What is it, honey?" my mom asks.

"You know Trevor?"

"Yeah, what about him?"

"He invited me to go see that new *Guardians of the Galaxy* movie with him. I know I've already seen it, but—"

"He asked you out?" my mom squeals, practically bursting my eardrums. "Oh my god, no way! You need to go get ready now. I'll call the hair salon, and we'll get you all pampered up and beautiful. You'll look gorgeous!"

"Mom, please. It's just a movie, and it's just Trevor."

"What do you mean it's 'just Trevor'? I always knew you two were meant for each other!"

"No, calm down. This is my night, and I really don't want to make a fool out of myself. I'm just going casual. I'm not a celebrity or anything."

"Fine, I guess I'll let you wear whatever ugly dress is in your closet."

A small gasp escapes my throat at my mom's hideous reaction. Why is she being so critical? "Are you serious? It's not like your clothes are any better! You obviously thought you were ugly too. Why else would you get all that Botox?"

"Ladies!" My dad's voice booms from the couch. I doubt he even knows what we're arguing about. He's probably just angry we're interrupting his golf show.

My mom inches forward and raises her voice. "Don't you dare insult your mother like that! I could've left you in that foster home, you know. We care for you every day. You need to be more appreciative."

I'm at a loss for words. I begin to break down in tears. I hate being vulnerable in front of my mom, but I can't even process how to leave this room. The tears are too uncontrollable.

"Aw, baby girl, don't cry," my mom says, returning back to her soft, squeaky tone. "I didn't mean it like that. I'm so sorry you took it that way. It was all just a misunderstanding."

"I'm sorry too." I choke over my tears. "I'm not trying to cry."

Feeling ashamed and embarrassed, I walk over to the stairs, and my mom goes back to scrubbing the counter tops. I wipe my face with the back of my hand and head upstairs.

When I make it to my room, I close the door behind me and sigh. I glance at my closet, knowing I should start getting ready. Trevor is going to be here in an hour. But I sulk over to the side of my bed and plop down. I gaze at the gray carpet, thinking about the argument with my mom. I shouldn't have criticized her fashion and plastic surgery. Of course, that would make her angry. She is a fashion designer, so technically, she knows more about clothing trends than I do. But still, she was making me upset. She never understands or even wants to understand where I'm coming from. It drives me insane.

I hear my phone buzz and pick it up. Trevor texted.

> Yo so im with some of my bros and were closer to ur house rn I thought it would be cool if they drove me to ur house and i could just pick you up sooner and they could drive us to the movies. That chill w you?

yeah thats totally fine! cant wait!!

I'll be there in about 30

I panic when I see his last message. I only have thirty minutes. I stand up quickly and rush over to my closet. I change into black skinny jeans and a teal tank top. I add a nice belt for flavor and step into a pair of black high-top Converse. When I get into the bathroom, I stare at my reflection for a minute. I think the outfit looks cute, so I don't know why my mom made such a fuss about it. Hopefully, Trevor will like it.

I brush through my long, thin dark hair. It's a little wavy, but I would curl it more if I had time. I apply moisturizer, concealer, foundation, powder, blush, highlight, mascara, and lip gloss as quickly as I can. I still have seven minutes left . I begin to grow anxious. I don't know why. I've known Trevor since third grade. It's not like this is the first time I'm meeting him. But at the same time, we didn't become friends until last year. Every time we were together was either at school or with other friends. This is going to be our first gathering with just the two of us. It's more intimate. I put on silver hoop earrings and a couple of silver and black bracelets. Then the doorbell rings. He's here. I try to take a deep breath and run down the stairs.

"I'll get it, Mom," I blurt out. I don't even know where she is right now, but I don't have time to care.

I open the door, and there he is, wearing the same outfit he wore at school.

"Are you ready?" he asks.

"You bet."

"You look gorgeous."

"Thanks!"

I follow him to his friend's black Chevrolet. Rap music blares from the radio. Trevor introduces me to his friends, Mason and Carlos. Carlos is the one driving. I hop in the back seats with Trevor. I find it interesting that I have been friends with Trevor for the past year, but he never mentioned these two guys. Maybe they're new friends of his, or maybe things are different now that we're actually dating. Maybe there's a whole different side to him I never saw.

"So, Trev, tell me more about this chic you've got with ya," Mason says, his long, blond, and fluffy hair blowing in the wind.

I stick my hand out the window and feel my smile growing wider. I have this feeling of adrenaline inside me, but it feels good, similar to the rush of energy I got on the golf cart a few months ago.

"I don't know. She's really something, I guess. I mean, we've known each other for years, and all of a sudden, she's started standing out to me more. She loves art and is weirdly into cold pizza."

"Really? That has to be part of my description?"

"What else do you want me to say?"

"Maybe that I love art, I have tons of cool friends, and I don't need someone else to describe my personality for me."

Carlos laughs, a clean smile spreading across his light brown skin. A curly strand of dark hair falls in his face. "She got you there, Trev. This is a good girl you picked out. You got approval from us."

"Yeah, man, we got you," Mason adds.

"Oh, I didn't know I had to get approved by some random dudes first."

I immediately regret saying that as soon as Trevor throws me a sharp look, almost with annoyance, but I can't tell. Why do I always ruin every good moment with him?

Then he softens his expression and whispers, "It's okay. Sorry, I just didn't want—Sometimes they can be a little sensitive. I didn't want them getting angry at you for calling them random, you know."

"Oh, sorry. I didn't mean to offend anybody."

"Whatcha guys whispering about back there, huh?" Carlos asks.

"Oooh! We got some lovers' gossip going on," Mason pesters with amusement.

"Bro, we're literally just on our first date," Trevor says. "Everyone, chill."

"Okay, and we're finally here," Carlos says as he drives us up to the theater entrance. "Hope you enjoyed your Uber. We shall see you at school tomorrow, our mighty Trev. Don't let the scary monster doesn't destroy y'all on the way back."

"Bye, thank you!" I cheer awkwardly, not knowing what else to say. The moment his friends are out of sight, I ask, "What was that all about?"

"Oh yeah, sorry. They can get really weird sometimes. Especially Carlos."

"Yeah, but who's the scary monster?"

Trevor laughs dryly. "That's my sister. They call her a bunch of different names. She's picking us up later."

"Oh okay. So, like, are these guys from class or . . . ?"

"Calm down. You're asking a lot of questions tonight."

"Sorry, I'm not trying to," I explain, feeling like I should say more but also scared of saying the wrong thing. I just want Trevor to be happy, but now I feel like I'm messing this entire date up. I hate how annoying I can get without even realizing it.

The smell of popcorn creeps up my nose the moment we enter the building. Trevor offers to pay for my drink and gets a bag of popcorn for us to share. He smiles and lets out a big laugh at the joke I make about the cashier. I feel more at ease now as we walk into the movie room together.

CHAPTER 6
LIVING IN A MOVIE

I sit up in my bed and check my phone. It's only 2:00 a.m. Why can't it just be morning already? I'm anything but tired. The adrenaline and butterflies are still lingering inside me. Trevor held my hand during one of the scenes. It was so adorable. The soft touch of his hand on mine made me melt with joy. I decide to text Trevor since I can't stop thinking about him.

> r u up?? i cant sleep

I shift positions and wait for him to text back. I wait. No response. I wait some more. Still no response. I should've known he's sleeping. I heave a deep sigh. The way Trevor looks at me makes me smile. If only I could see his face now. His warm hazel eyes are like deep pools of caramel. I imagine what it would be like to swim in them. My eyes begin to close when I feel a buzz against my stomach. Finally! He responded.

> i cant sleep either

> how weird! wanna go for a walk?

> That sounds perfect! Where are we meeting?

> south broad

Great! Cya :)

My first two dates in one night. How cool is that? I guess this isn't technically a date, but who cares? I wince my eyes as I turn on the bathroom light. When I adjust to the brightness, I fetch my hairbrush and comb through my delicate hair. I add some lip gloss and mascara to freshen up my looks. Then I grab a navy hoodie to wear over my black tank top and change into gray exercise shorts. I quietly tiptoe past Violet's and my parents' rooms and sneak out the back door, down the driveway, and onto the street.

I feel vulnerable, walking by myself in the middle of the night. Especially as a small teenage girl. At least I have my phone. If anything bad happens, I can always call Trevor. Although it's not cold, I still shiver. I hug my arms tightly and peer over my shoulder every couple of seconds. I know my parents don't care much about me, but I'm still scared they'll wake up and find me gone. I don't want to argue with my mom again. I hate it.

I finally reach the park entrance and search for Trevor. I spot him standing right next to the pavilion. Other than us, the park is empty.

"Hey," his calm, crisp voice whispers in my ear, "so aren't you gonna get in trouble, or what?"

"No," I stutter nervously. I'm still shivering, but I try to hide it. "I mean, if my parents wake up, I might, but I doubt it."

"Sneaking out to see your boyfriend, huh?"

"Oh shut up!"

We turn away from the picnic tables and head down a narrow, winding pathway. The light of the lamppost gleams against Trevor's face. I'm staring at his lips, thinking about how much I want to kiss him.

"D'you think I'm hot?"

"What?" I question, startled.

"You're staring at me 'cause I'm hot, right?"

I hit his arm playfully. He is pretty hot, but I'm not going to say that.

"Look who's blushing!"

"We are in the middle of a park! Anyone can hear us."

"Anyone? What dork would be following us at three in the morning?"

We both laugh for a minute before an awkward silence fills the air.

"Any news on Sadie?" he brings up.

"What? Oh, no. If I'm being honest, I actually forgot about the whole Sadie situation."

"Hmm."

"I don't know. I guess I'll try and see if I can figure anything out, but also, like, I'm probably just being paranoid."

"Hmm."

"C'mon, actually listen to what I'm saying!"

"Hmm."

"Trevor!" I yell while giggling.

"You're cute when you laugh."

I blush, and the silence is back again. He nudges my elbow, and I nudge him back. As we continue, I get this sudden urge, as if something's pushing me. I impulsively press my lips against his. Oh my god, I can't believe I'm actually kissing someone. His lips are a little chapped, and the taste of his saliva isn't pleasant, but I still continue kissing him. Then he lets go.

Trevor glances at his phone and states, "It's getting late. We should head back."

I'm sad I can't hang out with him longer. He makes me feel safe. I glance at my phone, and am shocked to see it's already 4:30. I have to hurry back before Mom wakes up.

"Okay, yeah, I guess we should go now," I say. "Thanks for tonight."

"No biggie. It was fun! See you tomorrow!"

I'm sprinting so fast I nearly trip over myself multiple times. We kissed! I can't believe it! We actually kissed! It was a little awkward, but it was our first. We'll get better over time. I want to scream; I'm so happy. I race over the fence, and this time I go through the basement so Mom and Dad can't hear me. I fly up the stairs to my bedroom. When I close the door, I collapse to the ground and take several deep breaths to balance my heart rate.

I take out my phone as I make it back to my bed to see a message from Trevor.

Thanks for the walk tonight see ya in a couple hours!

Hopefully you get some rest

At the end of the message is a red heart emoji! That's it. I'm officially in love.

I fall asleep thinking about the kiss. It was like a dream. This is something I'm going to remember for the rest of my life. My childhood crush is now my boyfriend. He's so sweet and innocent and caring. I feel like I'm living in a movie. This is insane, but I also love it at the same time. For once, I'm actually glad to be alive.

CHAPTER 7
A PAINFUL BLUR

'm at the lunch table with my friends, but Sadie has yet to show up. She's been late to everything this week. I'm not sure why. She said she was fine, but I'm still worried. She's my best friend, and I'm scared something might be going on with her. I want to help, but I don't know how.

"Hey, Spencer," I call out. Maybe he knows more information since the two of them are dating. At least I think they still are. "Has Sadie told you anything?"

"What do you mean?"

"You know, anything weird . . . about what's going on with her right now."

"No, I don't know. She's been more distant from me lately. I'm not sure why."

"Cal, I thought we talked about this," Trevor enters the conversation. "You need to stop overthinking this whole thing. It's stressing you out."

"I know, I know. I just want to know what's—"

"Well, I don't know. Sadie hasn't wanted to talk to me as much, and every time I try to plan something, she just—"

"I just what?" Sadie interrupts from behind us.

Shit. My jaw grows tense as I bite down on my left cheek, wondering how much of our conversation she heard. I don't want her to think I started the gossip. I mean, I kind of did but for a good reason. It appears I'm not the only one she's keeping secrets from. Maybe she also has her reasons. But I can't get rid of that gnawing feeling in my stomach. We've been caught. My teeth now clamp down on the side of my tongue. I want to stop destroying my mouth, but I can't.

"Oh, nothing."

"Spencer. Tell me."

"I said it's nothing."

"Cal, can you please tell me what's going on?"

"Not until you tell me what's going on," I say, the aftertaste of those words spiraling into an aching regret.

"I don't know what you're talking about."

"Why have you been so late to lunch? Why do you disappear all the time and lie about where you've been or what you've been doing? Just tell me. Please. Friends are supposed to tell each other everything."

There is a long, uncomfortable silence. I can feel the burning gaze of nearby students piercing through me.

At last, Sadie explains herself. "My mom. She . . . she has a new boyfriend. And I hate him so much. He keeps influencing my mom's issues and manipulating me and my brother to think that we are the bad ones. He just makes everything worse. It keeps causing me to have panic attacks. That's the truth."

She isn't lying this time. Eyes are the key to the soul, and as I look into hers, I know she's telling the truth—the real truth. I'm starting to think everything is fine and that we're all friends again, but Sadie opens her mouth for a second time.

"Why can't you accept the fact that not everything has to be said in public like this? What did you think I was hiding? Some plan to hurt you? Also, friends don't have to tell each other everything if they don't feel comfortable."

She storms out of the cafeteria, throwing her lunch tray on the floor. A random student screams, "Bitch!" at her after a whole cup of ranch dressing splatters across his shirt. Students who were staring at us turn their heads back around, pretending they didn't notice a thing. What the hell have I just done? I want to cry. My face heats up. I look at the ceiling to push back the tears, but I can't. A thin layer of water forms a shield around my eyes. My vision goes blurry. Blood swims around my tongue and I swallow it, the sharp taste burning my throat. I can't bear to look at anyone right now. I walk quickly out of the lunchroom in silence.

"Cal, wait! Where are you going?"

I drown out Trevor's voice. I am such a mess-up. I humiliated Sadie in front of everyone. What kind of friend am I? Will she ever forgive me for what I did? What if she never wants to be my friend again? If only I had thought about what I was going to say before I let it all out. This all could have been on Spencer. Sadie wasn't even mad at me; she was mad at him. She turned to me when he didn't give an answer. She trusted me enough to give her an honest response.

I turn down another hall on my way to the bathroom when I notice Trevor running behind me. I guess I should talk to him. He might make me feel better. I stop walking and turn around to face him.

"I hate myself," I mumble.

"No, don't say that. You're amazing. I just don't understand why you got on Sadie like that. Now you'll end your friendship and maybe me and Spencer's."

I feel hurt by his words. He can get pessimistic at times, but I also understand where he's coming from. Spencer is his closest friend, and if I just destroyed that bond, then he definitely has the right to be mad at me.

"Friends get in arguments sometimes. I'll make it up to her. I'm just so scared that I ruined everything. But I don't think there's going to be a problem with Spencer. He never got angry or anything."

"True, but the entire cafeteria saw."

"Why am I so stupid?"

"I know. Everyone's going to hate you now."

"Wow. That's comforting."

"That's not what I meant. I just don't want that to happen, and that's why you shouldn't have done what you did. That doesn't mean I'm not on your side."

I don't respond. I lean my head against his shoulder as we continue walking down the hall to find a place to sit. I knew there would be drama in high school, but I didn't think it would be like this, especially only during the first couple of days.

I catch a glimpse of Carla and Teresa walking toward us.

"There you are," Carla says.

"So you still wanna be my friend?" So much for being popular.

"Why wouldn't I?"

"Because I was a jerk for yelling at Sadie . . . in front of the whole cafeteria."

"That's not how I see it," Teresa adds. "Sadie was a jerk for not communicating with you, for making you feel like something bad was happening. And to be honest, I don't think everyone was paying attention."

"Yeah, but it was enough," I mutter under my breath.

"I think there was just a miscommunication error with everyone," Carla says.

"But it's going to be okay. You have us."

"I guess."

What puzzles me the most is Carla's attitude. Why is she being so nice? We aren't even that close of friends. What reason does she have to care for me? It could all just be an act, but I don't know.

"It's okay," Trevor soothes, rubbing my shoulder. "We're still your friends."

Lunch ends, and as I head to math class, I feel like everyone is watching me. I keep making accidental eye contact with people. I feel so awkward and exposed. I can't stop thinking about the way so many students looked at me at lunch. I bite my cheek as an attempt to rid myself of this uncomfortable feeling. I probably deserve the hate, but why didn't Sadie just tell me about her mom? We've been friends for nine years. What reason did she have to hide from me now?

I'm sitting on the hallway floor, staring intensely at my phone even though there's nothing to look at. All I'm trying to do is avoid everyone. The wall against me is cold and hard. The corner of a locker is stabbing my shoulder blade. I don't care. I'm already suffering on the inside.

I never wanted people to hate me. I thought high school was supposed to be fun, but all I want to do is cry. I keep telling myself it's okay. Things have separated Sadie and me before, and we always worked it out in the end. That's going to happen this time. It has to. Out of the corner of my eye, I notice someone stop directly in front of me. I look up from my phone to find Spencer looming over me. By the clenching of his fists and his aggressive stance, I can tell he's really angry. Like really, really angry. Trevor was right. I'm not ready for this. My body stiffens as I stand up.

"What is it?" I question, trying to sound tough, but my voice is obviously shaking.

He's struggling to find words. Finally, he stutters, "It's all your fault."

"Everything's my fault now. What did I do this time?"

"Sadie hates me. She's angry because she thinks I started gossiping about her behind her back all because you asked me earlier what was happening with our relationship."

"That's my fault? Wow. I thought you were smarter than that."

"And I thought you were smarter than that!" I've never heard him yell this aggressively. I shudder and try to take a step back but there's no room. "What the fuck, Cal. Sadie was right. You just can't stay out of anyone's fucking business."

I feel the tears rising again as he starts to walk away, but in a harsh flash of rage, he turns back around and slaps me across the face so hard I begin to feel numb. It takes a minute for the pain to kick, for my body to process my surroundings and what just occurred. Humiliation wraps around my throat like vines tightening around an old tree. The vines of shame carry me back down to the floor. Tears flood from my eyes, pouring out like a waterfall. I feel embarrassed, shocked, and angry at the same time. Students walk by me, but they become a blur. I can't stop crying, no matter how hard I try.

I hate Spencer. I also hate myself for not responding back with strength. I feel so weak and worthless. The first week of high school is coming to a close and so many people hate me now.

Teresa appears from around the corner. The moment she sees me, she rushes over. "Oh my god, Cal! What happened? Are you okay?"

The painful humiliation worsens. I was trying to avoid being seen. More tears fall down my face. I can't form an answer.

"Spencer hit me," I finally cry out. I feel so stupid.

"What? Are you serious? Why?"

"He's angry because he thinks I'm the reason Sadie broke up with him."

"What a fucking asshole."

Trevor is walking down the hall when he notices us. "What the hell is going on here?"

"Spencer hit her," Teresa explains in a bitter tone.

I can't even bear to look Trevor in the eyes. It's one thing for Teresa to see me in this state, but Trevor . . . God, now I feel weak.

"Spencer? Are you sure? He would never do that."

"But he did."

"I can't believe he'd do that. He's my friend."

"People aren't always what they seem."

"Do you think we should take her to the nurse's office?"

I shake my head. "I just need some time."

"Maybe get an ice pack if there is one," Teresa suggests. "Her face is a little red and flushed."

Great. Even the color of my face is screaming shame. How lovely.

Trevor glances at his phone and replies, "I don't know if I have time. My sister is here now, but you can take my water bottle."

Trevor hands Teresa his black CamelBak. I take it from her and place it against my right cheek. I didn't realize how hot my face was until now.

"I'm sorry. I'd normally stay, but my sister—"

"It's okay," Teresa says. "Don't feel bad. I get it."

"Thanks. Cal, I love you, okay? Text me later to let me know how you're doing." I nod, feeling miserable as he walks away.

"Okay, but before we leave today, we have to go to the principal's office to explain what happened," Teresa says. "What Spencer did is literal harassment."

"No, no. I don't need more pity."

"It's not about that. He needs punishment."

Only a second later, Carla shows up.

She asks the burning question. "Is everything okay?"

"Long story short, Spencer was an asshole and hit her in the face," Teresa says.

"Oh my god, that's horrible! Is there any way I can help?"

"Honestly, I've got it. We're just sitting here until she feels better."

"I'll join you!" she exclaims. "No support is ever too much."

On a normal day, I would attest. Sometimes excessive support can become overwhelming. But today is not a normal day, and although I don't want to admit it, I appreciate Carla taking time out of her afternoon to sit here and do her best to comfort me.

After a moment of silence, Carla says, "It's interesting to see the hallway from this perspective, you know. It reminds me of how big the world must look to a dog or something."

"Oh yeah, that is interesting. I've never really thought of that."

"I feel like such a terrible person. Trevor is going to hate me now," I sniffle.

"Why do you think that?" Teresa asks.

"Because Spencer was his best friend. And I just ruined their friendship."

"He'll get over it after a while. Spencer was obviously not the most stable person, so it's good they won't be friends anymore."

"Okay . . . I don't know how I'm gonna pay y'all back for your help."

"You don't need to do anything," Carla says with a beaming smile. "I'm choosing to be here with you."

There's a buzz, and Carla picks up her phone. "My mom is calling. Wait a sec. Hi, Mom. What's up?"

Pause.

"Yeah, sorry. I'm actually gonna be home a little later than normal. Calypso got hurt, so I'm helping her."

Pause.

"Yeah, I'll tell you more about it when I'm home later. I'm just trying to help right now."

Pause.

"I know, yeah. I hope so too."

Pause.

"Okay, I will. I'll text when I'm leaving here."

Pause.

"Love you too!"

The one thing I notice during Carla's conversation with her mom is how comfortable and happy she sounds. Carla is the first friend I've had who seems to have a good relationship with her parents. She is also the first person I know who has been so willing to help without me doing a single thing. I used to think she was weird and annoying, but I never really tried to be friends with her. I only saw her from a distance and made assumptions. This just comes to show that you never really know someone's true heart until you let them in.

CHAPTER 8
FACING FEAR . . .
AND SILENCE

I arrive at home extremely nauseous and exhausted. after sitting with Carla and Teresa for ten more minutes at the school, my face cooled down enough. I checked my reflection in the bathroom mirror before leaving. My cheek was still a bit red where he hit me, but it wasn't as bad. Teresa could not stop insisting I needed to go to the principal's office with her, but he already left before we got there. Hopefully we can talk to him next week, so Spencer can get the discipline he deserves.

Thank God my parents aren't downstairs when I enter the house. The last thing I want is for them to interrogate me about why I'm home later than normal. Spencer's face flickers in my mind. The way he cowered over me as if I were an object to be stomped on. Then the hostility in his body as he slapped his palm across my face. I wince remembering the sharp, extreme emotions of the moment. I feel tears traveling up to my eyes. The water begins to gather at the edge, but I do my best to breathe them back in.

I continue up the stairs to my bedroom, drowning in embarrassment. I hate myself. I ruined everything. I should've known it was drama with Sadie's parents. I have to remind myself I don't live in the midst of a suspenseful mystery movie, just the boring life of Brevard. I know I'm not the one to blame for what happened, but technically, if I hadn't made such a big deal about Sadie's attitude, she never would have gotten angry, and

Spencer wouldn't have hit me, and I would never have this disgusting mark of shame towering over me.

What makes the whole situation worse is that Spencer and I were friends. When he started dating Sadie, we grew close. Not as close as him and Trevor or him and Sadie but close enough. It's one thing for a random bully to hit you, but Spencer and I had a friendship. I feel exposed. He saw me crumble. He saw me weaken. His perception of me is now dumb, stupid, and weak. That's not the girl I wanted to be labeled as within my first few days of high school. I know I shouldn't care about what he thinks of me. We'll probably avoid talking to each other from now on. It's not just that. I had happy memories with him. Thinking about those happy memories now makes me cringe on another level. Why did I ever smile around him? This is the guy who slapped me in the face for something I didn't do. And Sadie didn't tell me everything about their relationship. Who knows how he actually treated her? Considering how his dad treats him and his mom, I wouldn't be surprised if this wasn't the first time Spencer has lashed out like this.

I finally decide I can't sit here and bask in my negativity any longer. I'm going to apologize to Sadie. In person. I have to think it through first, so I grab my phone and earbuds and blast music. Suddenly, an amazing idea comes to my mind. I quickly fetch a piece of paper and my special Bob Ross pencil. Then I scribble down my favorite things about Sadie. This will remove all the dismissive thoughts out of my head and help me summon up the courage to talk to her.

Here's what I write:

* *Her determination and perseverance*
* *How she always seems to know what's best for me before I do (she knew Trevor and I were perfect for each other before me)*
* *Her funny smirk when she gets excited about something*
* *Her thoughtfulness and care towards her little brother*

* *Her strength to keep smiling although she's going through so much*
* *Her love for dance*
* *She has a memory wall of pictures and items having to do with her favorite moments (I'M IN SO MANY PICS!!!)*
* *Her fun T shirts*
* *She's my BFF!*

What am I still doing huddled up in my bed when I have business to attend to? I feel a little nervous, but the only way to get rid of fear is to face it. I trot downstairs, snapping my fingers to the beat of my favorite song when I notice the house goes completely still and silent. That's odd. I stop snapping and look around. Maybe I'm just overthinking it, but the silence is so heavy. When I snap again, I realize nothing is wrong. Mom and Dad were still in the office and are walking down the hall now. That's why everything must have seemed so quiet. It freaks me out a little, but clearly, it was all in my head.

I wander out the door, the afternoon sun hitting my face. I look down at the ground in shame. I know I'm supposed to apologize to my friend and be free of negative thoughts, but it just doesn't work like that. I can't force myself to feel a certain way no matter how hard I try. I have forgiven my best friend, but I still haven't forgiven myself. The question is, will I ever be okay again? I should be. My moods are like a roller coaster. One day I'm sad; the next day I'm glad. I'm sure, after Sadie hears my apology, we'll be two peas in a pod again. Everything is going to be okay.

I am now on Sadie's front porch, ringing the doorbell. Her brother answers, and I ask if Sadie is there. He mumbles a quiet yes in his squeaky, pre-puberty voice. I stand there awkwardly, shifting my weight from one foot to the other, waiting for her to appear.

"Hey!" I say, trying to smile when she reaches the door. She immediately closes it behind her.

"Hey. What's up?"

"I just wanted to say I'm really sorry about what happened today. It was wrong of me to yell at you in front of the whole cafeteria. I feel terrible, and . . . I don't know. I guess I just—"

"It's okay."

I notice her eyes are red-rimmed with large dark circles underneath. I can tell she's been crying for a while, which is understandable. But it also looks like she hasn't slept in ages.

"You wanna go to the back porch and hang out?" Sadie asks. "You know, so we can fix the awkwardness between us."

"Of course! I would love that!"

She smiles at my response. I am so relieved everything is back to normal. I'm telling you, Sadie is the greatest friend anyone could ever have.

CHAPTER 9
SECRET POWER

A few weeks have passed by. I've gone on three more dates with Trevor, and our relationship is blossoming. Sadie and I are close friends again. A couple of nights ago, she slept over at my house, and we were discussing how odd our last sleepover was. This time we stayed up until 2:00 a.m. and I could tell we were both having a blast.

The principal found out what Spencer did to me, and he was punished with a week of out-of-school suspension. When he returned, he started hanging out more with the "edgy, rich, cool guys" group, which kind of makes sense. Spencer definitely has the most money compared to the rest of my friends. And a couple of those guys live in his neighborhood. But I thought he didn't want to be a rich snob like his parents. I guess he doesn't care now. I guess he'd rather fit into his true demeanor if it means having more friends.

All this drama has actually hit the hardest on Trevor. He and Spencer were really tight, and now they can't hang out anymore. At first, Trevor was assuring me nonstop that Spencer was just going through a rough spot in life and thought he should help him. I told him Spencer is toxic, and we should distance ourselves from him entirely.

Fortunately, Trevor and I are now on the same page. He might still be mad at me, but at least we're in agreement. Because of this, Trevor has grown closer with his other guy friends. For some reason he doesn't like me being around them. I think it makes him uncomfortable. I admit it makes me sad because his friends get in the way of our plans.

But I respect his choices and feelings.

Nala and Teresa have been talking more the past few weeks, staying up late on FaceTime with each other. A day or two after the drama with Spencer, Nala introduced us to her older brother, Kyle. He is really sweet, and for a week we sat with Nala and a few of the other senior boys. But Nala is now fully part of our friend group instead of always clinging to her brother. Last week, Nala confirmed she is lesbian, but unlike Teresa, she's more open about her sexuality, and her family is very accepting. after that, Teresa pulled me aside and asked if I could help set the two of them up on a date. I told her I don't have to be their middleman and that Teresa should have a conversation with Nala on her own. I understand why she's nervous to make a move. Teresa figured out she's bi only a couple of months ago. She's not very confident in her identity yet.

Carla and I have been spending more time together recently. Every weekend or so, we go to The Outlets or Rockin' Bowl. The Outlets is an outdoor mall in the center of Brevard. It has a lot of fun shops and restaurants, including Sadie's favorite, the Square Root. Rockin' Bowl is a bowling alley near The Outlets. Carla loves bowling and practically beats me every time, so I'm making it my mission to win. I personally enjoy bowling with her more than shopping or going out to eat. It gives us an activity to do, and we don't have to always worry about having a deep conversation. The two of us are very different, and I still don't quite understand her, but I'm beginning to enjoy her presence more and more.

Sadie, Trevor, and I are currently walking into the cafeteria to meet up with Carla, Teresa, and Nala. All the students' faces are busy gazing at a newspaper. Every fall a few of the seniors put together the Brevard High School newspaper. It's been a tradition ever since the school opened. The information in them is usually stupid and boring, but for some reason everyone is intrigued by this year's news.

"What's so interesting about the paper?" Trevor asks.

I am thinking the same thing. Nala flops the black-and-white paper in our faces. I rip it out of her hands, ready to read the latest senior gossip.

On the front, along with the heading, is a list of the students on the newspaper committee.

Andy Baxter

Erik Clayton

Josie Fox

Violet Gresham

Isaiah Hendrixx

George Lamb

Brittany Lester

Leah McGulsen

Parker Williams

The first thing I see when I open the page is a picture of two men in suits. What's so exciting about them? I analyze the picture more in an attempt to solve this mystery. The man on the left is tall with short brown hair and light beard stubble. The cleft on his chin is very prominent, and he has sharp brown slits for eyes. The other man is shorter and more fat than his companion. He has the thinnest lips I've ever seen and a large "anger T" on his forehead. I can tell by the lighting that the picture was taken at night. I catch a glimpse of the high school football field behind them. I move my eyes from the picture to the story below.

THE BATTLE OF POWER

This is a picture of the owners of the Deal and Do Company, Raymond Macon (left) and Daniel Smith (right). Their base headquarters are located here in Brevard, on Elm Bend Road to be exact. They are on the hunt for female freshman, Calypso

Gresham. She holds a special power that can stop the entire universe. The members of Deal and Do declare this power is very dangerous and if they are unable to capture her soon, she will continue to hold these powers. Who knows what actions she is capable of performing with them. The Deal and Do must stop her. The leader of this important business, Raymond Macon, declares, "That girl holds the thing we want most and we will stop at nothing until she is dead. The stronger her power grows, the stronger she becomes. And the stronger she becomes, our chances of survival weaken. We never give up. So, Calypso, watch out! We're coming for you."

Three more paragraphs follow that, but I can't bear to read more. At the bottom of the page is a picture of me, and under it is my name. I feel a cold shiver crawl down my spine, like a hairy tarantula scurrying across a carpet. I can't breathe. My lungs tighten, and my stomach clenches along with my jaw. This can't be real.

Trevor, who was reading over my shoulder the whole time, says, "Your sister must know about this. She's on the newspaper committee."

"So? Everyone knows now."

I take my attention away from him and begin to zone out. I keep staring at the picture of Raymond and Daniel until every single detail is forever implanted in my brain. They were at my school. Those horrifying men were at my school.

"If she knows about this, you could go talk to her and figure out a way to escape." Why is he still talking? It's obvious I've exited the conversation.

"You're kidding, right? I never talk to my sister. The only thing I know about her is that George Lamb is her boyfriend, she's a cheerleader, and when she was nine, she thought she was going to be a mermaid."

"Okay, I was just saying."

"Maybe you can help me."

"How? I know nothing—"

I stand on my tippy-toes and kiss his lips softly.

Teresa and Nala return with their lunch trays, hands interlocked. I look around, realizing Sadie and Carla aren't with us anymore.

"Crazy, right?" Nala emphasizes. "Who even are these lunatics? The Do and Shmoo."

"I have no idea," I say. "But the fact that they know more about me than I do creeps me out. Where are Carla and Sadie?"

"Bathroom," Teresa replies.

"Hmm."

"C'mon," Teresa urges. "You can't just stand there acting like this is all normal. We need to make a plan."

"Yeah, I know. Let's have the six of us hang out at . . . Carla's house after school, and we'll figure it out then. Is that good?"

"Yeah, that's fine with me. We just gotta make sure Carla's good with it."

"Yeah, I'll ask her later."

Nala makes some weird joke, and the two of them begin to laugh hysterically. I draw my focus to Trevor. He's wearing a grim face.

"I don't wanna die," I whisper in his ear so only he hears.

"You're gonna be okay, Cal. We'll figure this out. I have to head to Spanish now. I need to be there early to redo my test."

"Okay. Love you."

"Love you too."

I watch as he disappears within the wad of students at the end of the lunchroom.

"Y'all are so cute!" Teresa exclaims.

"Not as cute as you," Nala says.

"Oh, stop."

I ignore their bickering and stare at the floor, thinking, Why is life so hard?

⸝

I'm sitting on the floor of the library at Carla's house with Trevor, Teresa,

Nala, and Carla. Sadie has dance class on Thursdays, so she couldn't make it.

"I'm literally freaking out. How long have they been spying on me? How did the school find out about them? How did they find out about me? What if the whole army is behind that bookshelf right now?"

"Calm down. We're gonna figure this out. And besides, we would know if they were right behind us," Teresa says.

"Well, duh. I'm just saying. Why does this have to happen to me? I mean, do I really have some sort of powers? How do we know all the stuff they said was true?"

"I have an idea!" Carla proclaims. "Why don't we write down a list of all your strengths, then go from there? Maybe your power is just something you've been able to do really well this whole time but never realized because you thought it was normal."

"Good thinking," Trevor says. "I'm gonna go get myself some water. Be right back."

He seems pretty worried, so I follow him out of Carla's large and fancy library. It's filled with mounds of books, and a peaceful energy fills the air. Except today is different. I don't even remember what peace feels like at this point. I find Trevor standing in the hallway. The massive hallway. The walls are literally made of marble. I feel as if I'm inside a castle.

"What's wrong?" I ask as soon as we're away from everyone else.

I try to keep quiet since Carla's parents are also in the house.

"Are you clueless? You're in danger. Horrific danger. I want you to be safe." He rubs his sweaty palms through his auburn hair. "You're too young . . ."

"No. Don't say that. I'm even more worried than you. I want to live a long life. I want to be safe." Trevor's eyes begin to fill with tears, which makes me cry too. "Stop it. Don't cry."

"I'm not trying to," he sniffles. "It's just like . . . I already lost my mom. I can't lose you too."

"You won't. We are going to figure this out. We have to."

We both hug, and I wipe my tears on his blue striped shirt. The other three girls step into the hall and find us crying.

"Oh, guys," Nala says in a sympathetic tone. "It's okay. We'll figure this out."

"Group hug!" Carla squeals and practically throws herself on top of us. Teresa and Nala calmly join.

After we finish hugging, I get myself under control.

"The list, right? Let's get to it."

We are heading back, and Trevor mumbles in my ear, "Sorry."

"For what?"

"For making you cry."

"It's okay. I had to get those tears out eventually."

"Okay," Teresa declares as we sit down on the deep red carpet, "here's some paper. Now what are your biggest strengths?"

"Well . . . there's drawing. Definitely drawing."

They all glance at one another doubtfully, except Carla, who's twisting her hair with her pointer finger, only half paying attention.

"What?"

"Why would someone want to kill you if you had a drawing power?" Teresa inquires.

"What she's saying is," Trevor explains, "how would drawing be able to stop the universe?"

Stop the universe, I think. Those words remind me of something. Something that has barely crossed my mind until now. Last month, before I left to apologize to Sadie, I was walking down the stairs. Everything went completely silent. Completely still. But what did I do that made everything go silent and still? Then I remember. I had a song stuck in my head and was absentmindedly snapping to the beat. I was snapping. But the silence and stillness only lasted for a minute. What did I do to make it stop? I snapped again. Oh my god. That's terrifying. I think I just figured it out. Every time I snap, the world stops. Then when I snap a second time, it unpauses.

I thought that was a dream, but when I was seven years old, I was learning to snap, and when I finally learned how to, I kept doing it over and over. While snapping one day, I looked out the window and noticed a man walking a dog. He kept moving and freezing, then moving and freezing again. I pointed it out to my dad, but he told me it was just my imagination. That has to be it. That's my power. The reason I feel so confident about this statement is because it's almost as if my gut is nodding in confirmation. It's almost as if, deep down inside, I know and I remember I have these powers. I don't know how long I've had these powers. I'm assuming since birth. But where did they come from? Is that why my biological parents didn't want me? I'm not telling my friends about any of this. At least not for the moment. Not until I gain more information.

To test if my theory is true, I snap my fingers. Sure enough, the four of them, plus the rustling trees outside, freeze. But I'm still here. I'm not frozen. Nothing about me changes. At this minute I'm living in a world without any other living person or thing. Everything is frozen, even time. That's so freaky. I feel my breath go shallow. I quickly snap again. This is giving me too much anxiety.

"What just happened?" Carla asks.

"It was like we all blanked out for a second," Nala says.

"Yeah, I know. Cal, did you feel that?" Teresa questions.

"I . . ."

Thankfully, Trevor saves me with "I'm sure it was nothing."

"No, it was definitely something," Teresa states with thin lips. "Cal, did you—"

"I promise I didn't do anything. I don't know what just happened. I feel like I blanked out too."

"Calm down. It's okay," Nala comforts. "I'm sure we're all just tired from school."

"Why don't you go back to your house, Cal, and we'll talk more about this later?" Teresa suggests.

"But if you see or hear anything suspicious, let us know or hide somewhere if you can't reach us," Trevor adds.

"Okay, yeah. Thanks, guys."

"No problem!" Carla smiles.

"Also, Sadie lives right next door to me, so if I have a problem, I can always go to her house."

"Good idea," Trevor says.

All five of us walk into the hallway and out the front door toward our bikes. When we leave, Carla waves us goodbye and goes back into her house. Getting onto my bike, I feel different. I'm not the same person I was yesterday. Well, I am. It's just that yesterday, I didn't know who I was. But I feel way more out of place now than I did when I wandered around, clueless of my true self.

CHAPTER 10
LIES ON THE INTERNET

I creak the front door open with my key and make my way out of the pouring rain. My entire body is soaked. I wish I could tell someone about my powers, but I can't. How do I know they will keep it a secret? With this company wanting me dead for my powers, I can't risk telling anyone, not even my closest friends. It's so unreal that I can stop the entire world with just a simple snap of my fingers. The heavy silence and the complete stillness should soothe me, but it freaked me out at Carla's house. Even the trees stopped moving. I need to find out more information, so I head upstairs to my room.

Today is my parents' anniversary, so it's just me here with Violet. When I pass her room, I hear her loud, bubbly laughter. She must be on the phone with a friend. I'm debating whether I should ask her about the newspaper. after a minute of pondering outside her door, I decide not to. It's not like I need to. We rarely talk to each other in the first place, so what's the point? It's the same as telling a stranger on the street.

When I enter my room, I toss my heavy backpack against the desk. I scramble into my seat and open my laptop. I search "Deal and Do." All this junk about their new "missions" pops up. I'm scrolling past all the boring stuff—the history of the company, their most recent mission, their goals for the company. Blah, blah, blah. I go back to the search blurb at the top of my screen and type in "Deal and Do Calypso Gresham." It's scary how many articles with my name pop up. I click on the fourth link from the top, which takes me to what appears to be a personal website the Deal and Do members can post public announcements on. The paragraph below is short but a lot to take in.

> About 14 years ago, a girl now known as Calypso Gresham was born. She holds the power to stop the entire universe. With one small snap, she can pause the whole world and do whatever she pleases without anyone stopping her. Calypso has a background of attempting murder and if you let her take control, numerous deaths may occur along with other traumatizing events. There's only one way to put an end to this disaster and that is if Calypso is brought to our company, the Deal and Do. Our organization's goal is to save the world and make it a better place, and we can begin by eliminating this vicious criminal.
>
> Written by Raymond Macon,
>
> Leader of the Deal and Do Company
>
> Contact us at: 828-450-0038 or danandray@deal&do.org
>
> Or come visit our headquarter base: 3700 Elm Bend Road

Chills run down my spine. The air around me gets colder. The walls are inching closer and closer. There's no way I can go back to school tomorrow. after the newspaper came out today, several students probably searched the same thing I did, and now they'll actually think I'm a vicious criminal. Especially after they saw how I lashed out at Sadie last month. I'm not even sure how safe I feel in this town anymore. 3700 Elm Bend Road is just five to ten minutes away from my house. I don't go down that road a lot, but the times I have been there, I've only seen warehouses. Innocent warehouses. If only I knew how much danger was hiding behind those buildings.

The door opens and I whip my head around to find Violet standing at the edge of my room. Her wavy bleach blond hair and bright blue eyes resemble our mom greatly.

She's wearing a short white skirt and a light pink tank top.

I don't feel like talking to her at all. I don't feel like talking to anybody. Is my mouth even capable of forming words right now? Besides my raw cheekbones aching in pain, my throat feels like it's about to close up. Even though I shut the computer tight, I can still see the words "Calypso has a background of attempting murder" flashing on and off in my brain. I've never even thought about killing anyone. The internet lies all the time, but it's not just the internet; it's the people who want me dead. And it's out there for everyone to see.

"What's going on with you?" she questions.

"What's going on with you? Since when do we ever have a conversation?"

"I know. I've been busy."

"You've been busy? Wow, great excuse. Whatever. I don't want to talk to you."

"Well, I do."

"About what?"

"About . . . never mind. It doesn't matter."

"Tell me."

"It's just that you—I . . . uh. It doesn't really . . . I was just gonna tell you that I made some cupcakes earlier for you. Okay. I'm heading to Brittany's house now, so yeah. Okay, bye."

She rushes out of the room. What was her deal? Was it really that hard to tell me she made cupcakes? Why would she ever take the time to make those for me anyway? Why did she come into my room in the first place? Something is off with her, and I'm going to figure it out. I scurry down the stairs and into the basement. On my way down, I glance at the kitchen. There's no sign of cupcakes. Something is definitely off. I race into the backyard and sneak around the corner, watching as Violet walks briskly through the front lawn. Funny that she wouldn't get the car. It's almost as if she's making it easier for me to follow her. I hurry down the road and follow her footsteps into the dark and rainy night.

CHAPTER 11
A MYSTERIOUS CONNECTION

I quickly hide behind a bush. I feel like I'm the star of a horror movie, and the criminal is about to find out someone is following her. I've been trying to stay as close to Violet as possible without getting caught. I'm surprised she hasn't peered over her shoulder yet. The rain continues to splatter down onto the ground. It's pouring even harder now, making me regret wearing my beat-up white Converse. She takes a sudden turn at a dark corner hidden beneath the shadows. When I make it around the trees, a large white tent appears. I hear the low buzz of murmuring voices coming from the inside. Violet walks up to the entrance, and I step a bit closer, keeping myself hidden in the darkness.

A familiar guy in a tux greets Violet. It takes me a moment to place him, but I finally match the brown beard stubble and tall demeanor to Raymond Macon, leader of the Deal and Do. Raymond speaks in a rehearsed, professional tone. "Welcome. Inside are the rest of the members of the Deal and Do."

I am truly frightened. Did Violet act weird on purpose so I'd follow her into a trap? I hear a voice in my head telling me to run. I wait no longer. Next thing I know, I'm sprinting through the trees. Thorns and rough branches scrape my limbs. I finally make it out of the woods and arrive at a small trickling creek. Then it occurs to me I still have my phone. Someone could be tracking me, like Violet. Betrayer. We were never close, but I still feel hurt. I hear shouts and screams from behind me, so I quickly fetch my phone and send the link with the creepy article I read earlier to Trevor. With it, I say,

goodbye i'll miss you i love you

I was going to send a message to the rest of my friends, but the shouting and footsteps are growing closer. I toss my phone into the creek, and without looking back, I run for my life.

∽

I've been walking for what feels like hours. My feet hurt, my body aches, my mouth is dry, and I have no way to tell time. No phone. No watch. Nothing. I start crying heavily. I'm leaving Trevor. And Sadie. And Teresa. All my friends. Everything that's familiar to me. They're all gone. I don't even know where I'm going. How long until I stop running? I collapse to the ground, feeling helpless and hopeless. Leaning against a tree, I continue to choke over my tears. My loud and ugly cries echo throughout the quiet and empty atmosphere of the night. Who cares if the bad guys find me? It's not like I have anywhere else to go.

At least the rain stopped. But now I'm left wet, cold, and alone as I lie on the uncomfortable ground that I must call my bed. The grass is itchy on my arms, and a branch is poking into my back. I sigh heavily. The tree I'm leaning on rests at the bottom of a steep hill. Above me is the highway. I try to calm myself down as I listen to the rustle of the trees and the squeaky whoosh of wheels on the road. What has life become for me now?

I wake up to the sound of cars. I stretch my arms and yawn. My whole body throbs in pain. I've never experienced this way of living, at least that I can remember, but it truly is terrible. I woke up four or five times throughout the night not remembering where I was, and when I did, I began to cry again but returned to rest eventually.

The sun is rising behind the trees as I stand up and notice the silhouette of a person a few feet away from me. I don't know who they are or what they are doing here, but I feel as if a magnet is pulling me toward them. As if there's some sort of connection between us. This doesn't make sense. I don't know them at all. But again, nothing is making sense right now.

I haven't had any food since yesterday's lunch, which I only had two bites of anyway. The lunch at school tastes like crap, but right now I'd do anything for food, even if it meant a cold, rubbery burger. I'm starving, tired, confused, and lonely, so maybe this person could help. As I draw closer, I see a boy, who seems close to my age, maybe a year or two older. His dark curly hair is dirty and full of knots, almost like a bird's nest sitting on his head. His dark caramel skin is smooth and muscular, covered in a too-tight gray T-shirt and black joggers. What really shocks me is his eye color. His irises are an exotic shade of purple. They have to be contacts. No way those are real.

"Hello," I croak as I approach him, my voice sounding small and pitiful. "Do I know you?"

"No. I . . . um, was wondering if maybe you could help me."

"Me? Help a stranger? I don't think so. I don't even know your fucking name."

"Well, I could tell you. But only if you prove you aren't going to hurt me."

"I'm not going to hurt anyone unless I have to. Not unless you're dangerous."

"I'm definitely not dangerous. People think I am. I don't know why."

"Stop rambling and just tell me your name. That'll show me that you aren't dangerous."

"I am not rambling! And my name is Calypso."

"Okay, well, I'm Nate. Nice to meet you."

Nate . . . Nate. I don't know what it is, but I feel some sort of familiarity with myself and that name. A connection. But again, why would I feel a connection between me and a stranger I just met? Neither of us move, so I'm stuck staring at him with an awkward smile as he eyes me skeptically, trying to read my face.

"Um, so what am I supposed to do now?"

"Don't ask me. You were the one that came over here in the first place."

"Good point. I was wondering . . . if you could help me."

"Sure. There's someone over there," he says, pointing behind me. "They can help."

I can't tell who he's pointing at, so I turn back around to ask, only to find he's running away.

I chase after him, looking even more like a freak. "Nate! Nate, come back!"

When I catch up to him, he stops. "I guess you just can't leave people alone, can you?"

"Not until you help me. Please!" I beg. "I have no food, no water, no one to go to, no money, no nothing. Can I please come with you?"

"What the fuck," he mutters under his breath.

I guess I caught Nate on a bad day. He glares at me for so long I start to feel oddly exposed. Finally, with a dramatic eye roll, he says, "Fine. Follow me."

"Yes! Yes! Yes! You don't know how much that means to me."

"But one thing. Please don't shout my name in the streets for everyone to hear."

"Why? Are you in danger too?"

"Not necessarily. It's a secret."

"Ooh! I love secrets!"

"I never said I was telling."

The good thing is I'm not alone anymore.

CHAPTER 12
NATE

"This is where I stay," Nate declares.

In front of me is a broken-down, abandoned barn. The remains are brown with a red roof. Leading to it is a long, skinny, plant-smothered pathway with a mailbox at the end. Many trees surround the back of the area. I can't tell whether the empty hole in my stomach is from my strong need for food or the chilling presence of this place. Is this what I'll have to call home from now on? I can feel Nate's eyes studying my expression.

"You asked for my help, and I helped you. I never said we were going to a luxury mansion."

"Isn't this a bit weird, though? I don't even know who you are, and now I have to live with you."

My gut responds to that statement with a strange tug. I ignore it. I don't know Nate, and he doesn't know me. End of story. "It's better than dying."

"I guess," I mumble.

"Let's go inside, and I'll show you around my shithole of a home."

I sense bitter sarcasm in his voice. I know his comment is directed at me.

"I'm sorry, okay? I didn't mean to call your place shit. I'm just not used to this."

"Whatever. I'm not mad. Let's just move on."

I examine the barn with disgust. A couple bottles of water, some snack wrappers, and food cans are scattered about in the far right corner. To the left of the food and water are three small and dirty stables. To the left of me is a musty wooden table. It's going to take a while for me to get comfortable here.

"Why'd you run away in the first place?" he asks.

"I . . . I'm not sure if I can tell you. I don't know how much I can trust you."

"Well, you should probably tell me. I need to know how much danger we're in."

"Fine. But only if you tell me why you are living here and not in a real home."

"Okay, but after you tell me your story."

My gut does a little flip again. What the hell is happening? I continue to ignore it as I reveal, "I found out yesterday when I was at school that I apparently have some sort of powers I had never known about before. I also found out that this evil gang of villains wants to kill me. When I got home from school yesterday, I researched the company and found all these articles about me. The company is called the Deal and Do. I clicked on one of the articles, and all of these lies about me were on there. This dude from the company was saying how I had previously attempted murder, which I would never do in my life. It also said that if someone takes me to the company, they'll help, but I know they won't. I know they're lying."

Nate looks completely stunned and says nothing.

"Ugh, I should never have told you," I say, an overwhelming wave of guilt splashing over me. "I'm not supposed to trust anyone."

"No, you can trust me. We're actually in a similar situation."

I peer at him with a confused expression. "We are? How?"

"I have powers too."

It's as if my gut nods in approval. *So we are connected.*

"What do you mean we're connected?" Nate questions.

I look up, flustered. I didn't realize I said my thoughts aloud.

"Oh sorry. I just . . . The main reason I asked for your help earlier was because I had this weird feeling . . . that we are somehow connected."

"Me too. That's one of the reasons why I decided to help you."

We both stare at each other in silence. An excited feeling rushes through me. Is that adrenaline? Or fear? Or uncertainty? Probably all the above.

"What the hell?" Nate mutters to himself. He runs his fingers through his hair.

"This all sounds so fucking crazy. Like we're in a movie or something."

"I know, for real. So what is your power?"

"Basically, I can read people's minds. But only if I'm within ten feet of them. That's why my eyes are purple. The power juice is in my irises."

"Oh my god! That's so unreal!" I exclaim. "Can you see what I'm thinking?"

"No, I can't. I was trying to figure out why. I thought maybe there was something wrong with me and that my powers shut off. But now I know it's because you have powers too. That's another reason why I helped you—so that I could figure out why I couldn't read your mind."

"Oh my god. This is all so strange. I can't believe we found each other."

"What's your power?" he asks.

"I can pause the world with one single snap of my fingers and then unpause it with another snap."

"That's actually pretty sick."

"Yeah, it's weird though. I didn't believe it at first."

We gaze at each other in awe before he clears his throat and says, "Anyways. You can sleep in one of these horse stables. I'm in the one all the way to the right."

"Okay. Wait. Nate?"

"Yeah?"

"How come the company isn't after you as much as they're out for me?"

"They . . . um. They think I'm dead."

"Oh. Why?"

"It's a long story."

"Come on. Just tell me."

"Fine, I will. You ask a lot of questions," Nate says, gritting his teeth with annoyance.

"Sorry, I'm just new to this whole living-with-another-stranger-who-has-powers thing."

He actually laughs at that. "Okay, so when I was younger, I was abandoned by my biological parents. I honestly don't remember much of what happened—"

"Oh my god, same!" I shriek.

Nate throws me a strange look, but I ignore it. I have never met someone so similar to me.

"Weird. Anyways, this couple found me, and they took me in. Their names were Harper and Joe. They told me about my powers on my thirteenth birthday and—"

"They told you?"

"Yeah. Didn't your parents tell you?"

"No. Remember? I told you I found out at school. It was in the newspaper."

"Oh. Well, I'm not gonna go into all the messy shit, but the house caught on fire, and they didn't survive. after that, I knew I was in big trouble. I had no one to keep me safe from the people who wanted me dead. I had to stay low so they'd think I also died in the fire, which worked, I guess. I ran all the way until I found this barn."

"That's terrible. I'm so sorry."

"Don't be. It was a long time ago."

"How long has it been since you found this place?" I ask.

"Well, I was thirteen, and now I'm sixteen, so that was three years."

"That's a long time. At least now you have someone else with you."

It feels great to have a distraction from all the sadness and fear I'm experiencing after running away. Nate and I have so much more in common than meets the eye. We both have powers, we were both adopted, we both are in danger from the Deal and Do, and we both ran away from home. I think we are going to get along just perfectly.

CHAPTER 13
MIRACLE

I stare at the tall evergreen branches and let my mind wander. I'm sitting on a tree stump outside the barn, soaking in the refreshing atmosphere of nature around me. The temperature is cooler now that fall is almost here. Good thing I was wearing a jacket when I ran away. Otherwise, I would be freezing in just my tank top and leggings.

Nate is out on a run. It's a part of his daily routine. He asked if I wanted to come with him, but I hate running. It takes way too much energy and motivation. Plus, I am not going to embarrass myself in front of Nate.

The past couple of days have been dull and boring. It's not easy adjusting to this new lifestyle. Hell, it's hard for me to even get used to Nate. Normally, I would see my friends throughout the day, then go home and charge my social battery with some alone time. Now I'm constantly with Nate, and I don't even know if I consider him a friend or not. I feel like there's a lot more to him, and it's all hidden beneath this thick wall of bitterness he's built. He has been living alone for three years, and who knows what his life was like before his parents passed away? He probably hasn't gotten a day to relax in years. And over those years, he's built a barrier around himself as a protective mechanism. I don't even know why I'm thinking so deeply about this. He's just a guy, and I don't know him. What right do I have to justify his actions?

I try to put my mind on something else, but I can't stop thinking about how unbelievable life is now. I don't know when or if I'll ever be able to go back home again. Nate has been out here for three years. Who knows how many more years we've got at this stupid barn? Yes, I'm not alone, but there's still an empty hole in my heart that Nate can't fill. What if I never get to see any of my friends again? I miss them terribly. I miss Trevor even more. Oh, what I would give to go on a late night walk in the park with him again. Just one more time.

My friends are probably worried sick about me. They have no idea where I am or if I'm even alive anymore. All they have is that message I sent to Trevor. But it was so vague. With the way I said goodbye, what if Trevor thought I was hinting at something else? I laugh at myself for even assuming my friends are worrying about me. Do they really care about me that much? They still have one another, and they're all going to school and living a normal life. What if they forgot about me?

I hate this. I can't help thinking about what would've happened if I didn't follow Violet. I would've had to run away eventually. Raymond and Daniel were already hunting me down. And with the newspaper and the article I found online, it wouldn't have been long before someone took me to the Deal and Do headquarters. This is what my life has become now—a constant cycle of worrying. I hate it. I hate everything. I can't even describe this anxious, angry weight I'm feeling right now. I begin to weep. This is so overwhelming; I can't take it. Why does everything seem to be turning against me?

All of a sudden, I hear Nate say my name. He's standing right in front of me. I didn't even notice him walking over. I quickly wipe my face with my hands and stop crying.

"What's going on?" he asks.

"Nothing. It's nothing. I'm fine. Sorry."

"It's obviously not nothing. What's going on?"

I'm surprised he didn't retort some snarky comment instead. Not only that, but he also sits down next to me. He actually cares. I can sense it in his voice, and that warms my heart.

"How did you do it? How were you able to stay alive and sane all those years in this barn?"

He scoffs and says, "I stayed alive, yes, but let's not assume I didn't go insane."

"Yeah, but, like . . . still . . ."

"Honestly, I don't know. I guess I just kinda took the whole thing one day at a time. But there were many days, weeks even, where I was going crazy because all I had was myself. And sometimes you just really hate yourself, you know. You need that other person there to keep you accountable. God, I still don't know how I've done it, how I'm still alive. But I am. And now you're here, and I know I haven't been the nicest to you, but you were a miracle. I've been waiting for someone to just magically show up, and here you are."

"I'm your miracle?"

"Well, not like that. Now you're making this weird."

We share a moment of laughter.

"So you feeling better now?" he asks.

"Yeah, actually, I am."

"I'm not usually one to cheer up someone's day."

"Aw, well, you accomplished your goal with me."

Nate chuckles at that. He stands up and asks, "You wanna head back inside now? I managed to get us a couple good snacks on the way back from my run."

"Really? How'd you get them?"

"Stealing is a necessary part of survival, just as long as you don't get caught."

"So you're a thief now?"

"No, I wouldn't say that. I'm just . . . skilled."

"Oh yeah, totally. Totally skilled," I say with exaggerated sarcasm.

We're walking up the small slope of a hill toward the barn when I notice the clouds are growing darker.

"It looks like it's gonna rain," Nate remarks. "So later we'll fill up our water bottles again."

"Oh yeah. I noticed they were getting empty earlier."

When we get back inside the barn, I grab a bag of chips for us to share. We sit near the stables and munch on our snack.

"How was your run?" I ask Nate to fill in the silence.

"Good. Would've been better if I had some company, though."

"I told you, running's not my thing. And aren't you used to doing it by yourself?"

"Well, yeah, of course I am. But I think you should try it out. Besides, we never know if the Deal and Do will show up here or something. We always need to be prepared to run."

"Yeah, but, like . . . I don't know. I just don't think I'm ready. I'm not good enough."

"You don't have to be. Everyone is a beginner at some point. See, I wasn't much of a runner until a month into me staying here. I needed something else for me to do other than just sitting around. And yes, I wasn't good at first, but I got better. It helps me clear my head and just get stronger, you know. Plus, it gave me something to look forward to. Every day I told myself I would do more than I did the day before. I competed with myself and made goals. That's what made it fun."

"Okay, fine. I'll go with you tomorrow."

Although I'm feeling more depressed than usual, Nate is a good person to be around during this new adjustment period of my life. He's motivating me to grow as a person. It's always good to have someone like that around you.

CHAPTER 14
SLOW AND STEADY WINS THE RACE

"We don't have to run that far. Just tell me when you wanna turn around."

"I probably won't even go over a mile," I say.

"And that's okay. Remember, everyone starts out as a beginner."

"You're good at this."

Nate smiles at my comment. "Well, I've had to train myself for so long."

After looking at Nate for another minute, I take a big, deep breath. "Okay, I've got this."

"Yes, you do."

I begin to run, and Nate stays next to me, even though I know he can go way faster.

"Remember to maintain a steady pace throughout. It's never good to use all your energy in the beginning."

"Okay."

"And don't scuff your feet against the ground. It wears you out more."

"I'm trying . . . not to," I say, already out of breath.

I do my best not to scuff my feet, but it's really hard. I feel like I'm dying. My lungs are burning, and my throat is dry. I stop.

"I can't do this," I grumble.

"Yes, you can. You just gotta keep going. Ignore the pain. Set your mind on something else."

"No, this is pointless, okay? Let's just walk back."

"C'mon, I believe in you," Nate affirms. "Try going down to that stop sign."

"But my lungs are burning, and my stomach hurts, and I think I have a cramp," I confess while placing my hand against my chest. My heartbeat pounds rapidly inside my body.

"Okay, just keep your breathing steady. Remember to inhale and exhale slowly. You've got this. There's no point in turning back now."

I take some deep breaths with Nate before I feel better again.

"Fine," I say. "We can run some more. But once I say we're turning back around, you better listen."

"Okay, I will."

We continue running. When we make it down to the stop sign, I don't turn around. I put all of Nate's suggestions into practice and see a bit of an improvement, although my pace is still quite slow.

"Nate, talk to me about something. To distract me."

"Um, okay," he replies, then tries to think of something. "What are some of your hobbies?"

"Ooh, okay, um . . . well, I love art. That was like my thing, you know. It sounds dumb, but I really wanted to be a famous artist. Obviously, that's off the list now."

"Why?"

"I mean, who knows how long we'll be in this barn?"

"That's true. We can only hope it's not forever. But hope is kinda stupid sometimes, don't you think?"

"Yeah, I guess. But I also feel like art is just a hobby of mine, and although I wanted that to be my career, I'm starting to think I won't enjoy it as a job. So I don't know."

"Oh, I see."

"I think I wanna turn around now," I say after a few seconds of silence.

"Okay, let's just go to the funny-looking tree up here."

"Okay."

When we turn around, Nate exclaims, "That was good! You made it farther than you'd thought."

"Yeah, I guess I did," I say, a smile spreading across my face.

"You seem pretty proud of that."

"That's because I am."

I really am proud of myself. Maybe this new life isn't so bad after all. Maybe this is a growing period that I very much needed. I'm already accomplishing something I never thought I would. Who knows how much more I'll accomplish in the weeks to come, maybe even months and years? Even though there's less hope, I am still so curious of what my future will look like.

CHAPTER 15
FIERY FLASHBACKS

Two weeks have passed, and I'm starting to feel more comfortable around Nate. Each day I wake up and feel more at ease than I did the day before. I'm sitting on my favorite spot, the tree stump. I love it here because I get a clear view of the landscape—the barn up to my right, a glimpse of the pond ahead of me, and the evergreen trees that provide security and isolation from the world around me. The world in which I have so much control over it scares me. The fact that I have the power to stop not only time but also the world itself makes me terrified. It's such a simple but complex thing at the same time.

My mind drifts over to Nate. He's told me a little bit about his backstory and how he feels about his powers, but he's never dived that deep into it. I wonder if he's scared of himself and his abilities like I am. At the same time, I figure he probably is more comfortable with them since he's known about them longer. He obviously had a good relationship with his adoptive parents, but I wish I knew more. I don't know why I crave the desire to discover more about Nate. Some feelings are too difficult to explain. That always seems to be the case with me.

As if on cue, Nate comes sauntering down the slope toward me. I look over at him and immediately smile. It's not a smile I can control; it just appears out of nowhere, and I can't stop it.

"You're up early again" is Nate's way of greeting me.

"Yeah."

"And I thought I was the early bird."

"I don't know. I haven't been able to sleep much lately. I mean, I've never really been a good sleeper. It's just worse now that I'm living in a barn."

"Insomnia?"

"Maybe. Who knows?"

Nate begins to zone out in silence.

I stand up. "Are there any snacks left in the barn?"

"I don't know. We can check. But remember, we have to—"

"Ration. I know."

I happen to find a bag of popcorn hidden in the corner. Not the most ideal breakfast, but it'll do. I grab my half-filled plastic water bottle from yesterday and gulp down a couple of small sips before munching on the stale, bland popcorn.

"So," I begin, trying to spark conversation, "why don't you tell me more about your parents?"

Nate scoffs. "What is this? Some sort of interrogation?"

"What are you so defensive for?"

"I don't know. I just thought it was a random question."

"I guess. I was just curious."

"Okay, fine. Um . . . their names were Harper and Joel. They adopted me when I was five. Before then I was just in an adoption center." "Yeah, I know all that. Tell me something new."

"Fine. So, um . . . they homeschooled me until fifth grade. They were really careful about making sure I stayed safe and was always around them, especially after they figured out about the Deal and Do. I'm not sure when exactly they found out about my powers and everything, but they definitely knew for a couple years before they told me."

"How interesting," I say. "It makes me wonder how much my parents knew about the Deal and Do. But honestly, if they did know, I'd be surprised if they even cared."

"Yeah, I don't know. Oh, but my mom was also a nurse, so instead of going out to the doctor's office, I counted on her to keep me healthy. I think the two of them just enjoyed the fact that they had a child. Harper had three miscarriages before I came along."

"Oh god, yeah. Then I can totally understand where they were coming from. You're lucky you were given a great set of parents."

"I felt very lucky until . . . you know, the fire happened," Nate utters, his voice beginning to choke up. This time, I don't interrupt him with any dumb comments. I let him take the time he needs. "And of course, the night was going pretty well before that. I was in my room, playing video games. My mom was making dinner downstairs. It was one of my favorite meals of hers, Dad's too. Her homemade stir fry. God, I can practically taste it now. It was so amazing.

"I don't know exactly what caused it to start. All I know is something happened in the kitchen. I couldn't hear anything through my headphones. It wasn't until some louder screaming came through, and I began to smell the smoke. I took my headphones off and rushed outside my room. I ran downstairs and found my dad trapped in the smoke and bright orange flames. He told me all I needed to do was get out of the house before it got worse and run as far as I could. I thought he'd come with me, but he went back in to save my mom. Obviously, they both didn't make it. And I continued running until I found this barn."

"Oh my god, that's so scary," I say, baffling at Nate's strength, both physically and mentally.

"Yeah, I know. And to make things worse, I didn't have any friends to go to. Even the neighbors hated me. My parents kept me homeschooled for so long that by the time I was thrown into public school, I had such a hard time making friends. Especially because they sheltered me away from the real world so much. Yeah, they were great parents, and I loved them, but sometimes I just wished they had let me live."

"No, I get you. That must've been so hard."

"Sometimes I wonder what my life would be like if Harper hadn't been making stir fry that night, if the fire hadn't started. What if my parents were still alive? I'd be living comfortably inside a real house with a real bed and sturdy walls and a roof and actual meals to eat."

"Yeah," I respond, trying to sound empathetic and sincere, but I feel like everything I'm saying is coming off as fake. "Sorry, I'm the one who asks you all these questions, but then I don't know what to say afterwards."

"You don't need to say anything. I'm just glad I can finally tell someone all this. For the past three years, I've been bearing the weight of all those painful feelings myself. I still feel so guilty for running away when I could've tried to save my parents." Nate's eyes finally begin to water as he croaks, "I didn't even try."

"There was nothing you could do. You were scared, and you just did what your dad told you to do, like a good son would."

"I know, but still . . ."

"But still what?"

"I don't know. I guess you're right. I did what my dad told me to do, and if they could see me now, I bet they'd be proud of how far I've come. But I just can't help but think about the alternative side to the situation, you know?"

I nod, completely understanding that feeling. There's always a "What if?" or a "But still . . ." trail for everything. It might not be right or healthy, but I take that route all the time. Why wouldn't I? Sometimes I can't control what my brain does.

CHAPTER 16
ABANDONED AGAIN

Today marks exactly one month and ten days since I ran away from home, but it feels like I've been gone for so much longer. It's difficult not seeing my friends and family. The first couple of weeks I was sad, but it still wasn't processing in my mind everything that had happened. My life went from normal to horrifyingly unreal in the span of one day.

The good thing is I have Nate. We weren't getting along as well at first, but now I don't know how I'd survive without him. He's the reason I'm still living and breathing. He didn't like to admit it at first, but I think he enjoys my presence too. We both found each other in our most scared and lonely moments. I think there's something special about that.

"Hey, Calypso," Nate says, getting my attention.

I'm sitting on the floor of the barn, my back leaning against the leg of the table. I look up and notice a folded piece of paper in his right hand.

"What is it?" I ask, now noticing the fear rushing through Nate's bright purple eyes.

I set down the can of soggy black beans, which is supposed to be my breakfast.

Nate hands me the paper, and I open it, afraid to see what's inside.

"I recognize the handwriting," I whisper as if we're around other people. "This is from my mom."

Calypso,

We know you're out there somewhere. Wherever you are, you need to come back. This is not a suggestion, this is a command. You know we love you and care for you, but this is going too far. When you come back, go to the Deal and Do Headquarters immediately. They can help you. If you've heard any bad rumors about them, those aren't true. We only want what is best for you. We miss you, honey bun, and we are sorry if we ever did anything wrong. If you need anything always remember we are here for you.

Much love,

Mommy and Daddy

"Where did you find this?" I tremble.

"In the mailbox."

"Since when do you ever look inside that old piece of shit?"

"It was open, and I noticed something was in there."

"I don't know how to feel about this."

He doesn't respond, so I spill my thoughts. "I'm not going back. Not unless I have to. It's too dangerous. Everyone at school thinks I'm a murderer. My sister is with those freaks. And I'm pretty sure my parents are too. Look at this."

I hold the paper in front of his face and point to the part about the Deal and Do and the rumors.

"Are they out of their minds? They think this is gonna make me listen to them? They're so stupid!"

"Your family sounds like a bunch of fake bitches. You're right. This is crazy. They're sugarcoating this whole thing with a bunch of 'I love you, honey buns' and 'We miss you, sweeties.'"

"Yeah, I know. I just don't know what to think. If I ever do decide to go back, I now have no one to go to. My entire family is part of the hate group that wants to kill me. And I've been away from my friends for so long. They probably think I'm dead. I just—" I am interrupted by a wave of hot tears. "I feel so lonely."

"It's okay to feel like that sometimes. It's valid."

I begin to lean my head on Nate's shoulder and cry, but he suddenly jolts up.

"What is it?" I ask, pausing my crying session.

"How did they find us in the first place?"

"They didn't. They—"

"They put it in that mailbox right in front of us. They have to know you're here. Which means . . ."

"Which means . . . what?"

"Let me see you," he demands.

"No, stop." I back away. "What are you gonna do?"

"Just come over here."

I walk towards him. He focuses his gaze at my clothes.

"What are you doing?" I start growing a bit irritated.

"Checking for a tr—Yep. Right there." He points to a tiny black circle on the edge of my black jacket sleeve. It's so tiny, I'm shocked he found it so quickly. I've never even noticed it before.

"What is that?"

"A tracker. What I thought." I can see the anger spreading on his face.

"But how? How did it get there?"

"Wait a second. Come closer."

I'm practically standing on top of him now, which is really awkward, but I have worse things to worry about.

"Dammit," he mutters.

"What is it now?"

"This isn't just a tracker. It's a tracker for Deal and Do. Your parents are with them."

"Exactly. But didn't we already know that?"

"To be fair, we assumed it, from the tone of the card. Your parents also could have genuinely been concerned for you and just blindly believed the Deal and Do was a good, trustworthy company like they promote themselves to be. But now we know for sure that they are part of the Deal and Do."

"How do you know it's actually a Deal and Do tracker?"

"Look at it." From the angle I'm at, it's pretty hard to see the details, but I trust Nate. "It says D&D on it. Deal and Do."

"Ugh, I just don't get it!" I can't help it, but another tear falls down my face, and before I know it, I'm sobbing. "Why would they want to do something like this? My parents. My sister. They all abandoned me. The people I've known for the longest time abandoned me. Like, seriously, Nate, is there something wrong with me?"

"No. You're an amazing person. I mean it."

"There must be something. I had parents. They abandoned me. I was alone, then adopted. Next thing you know . . . I'm abandoned again."

"I know, I'm so sorry. I really don't know what to say. I understand your pain. I've been alone for the past three years. But I'm always here for you."

He lets out his hands, offering a hug. But I push him away.

"I just need some time alone right now."

"Whatever you need," he says.

Then Nate stands up and grabs a dirty blue sweater that looks a bit large. He hands it to me. "Here. I found this outside the barn when I first arrived, but I've always just left it sitting over there. It's probably a good idea to change into something new."

I race out the barn door and toward the colorful red and orange trees. The fall breeze hits my wet, tear-smothered face. I inhale and exhale deeply, trying to steady my heart rate. When I make it to the edge of the pond, I yank the tracker off my jacket, tearing a bit of fabric with it. I place the small black circle on the ground, crush it with my foot, and watch as all the little pieces shatter around me. Then I bitterly toss my jacket into the murky water and twist myself through the sweater Nate gave me.

When I'm done wrestling into my new clothes, I sit on a rock facing the water. Looking up at the light gray blanket of sky, I watch a few rays of sunshine peek through, and I collect my thoughts. I let the rest of my tears flow freely down my face. I'm so angry that my life has to be this difficult. I feel like no one can truly understand what I'm going through. Only Nate knows because he's been faced with the same situation.

My energy is draining. I have to ration food and sleep on the stiff, frigid floors of the smelly barn. The matters I used to give no thought over are now a priority.

I begin to ponder over my parents as a small green spider crawls onto my leg. I lightly flick it off without killing it. How did the tracker even get on my shirt in the first place? I am thinking back to all the interactions I had with them right before I left. The first thing that comes to my mind is how fake my mother acted around me. I always assumed she was treating me like a baby because she was annoying like that, but it was always bigger than that. She was only trying to cover up her real story. She told me she was a fashion designer and that my dad was an insurance agent, but all along they were working for these Deal and Do snobs. That's where all their money came from.

Then it suddenly occurs to me. My mom and I may not have been close, but she knew me well enough to know I usually wear the first shirt on top of the stack in my dresser, except for on special occasions. The night before I ran away, she came into my room with a stack of clean clothing, and instead of sloppily throwing them on the floor and letting me do it, she said, "You've had a long day. Why don't I help you, baby doll?" I should've noticed, but she always acted weird around me, so I stepped into my bathroom and let her do her business. That was when she put the tracker on my shirt.

Regret is a terrible feeling.

CHAPTER 17
SECRET ESCAPE PLAN

We stop after running three miles. I lick the salty sweat off my chapped lips.

Although Nate has helped me gain more strength, running with him can be difficult.

His pace is way faster than mine, but he occasionally slows down to keep up with me. There are so many times I want to stop, but Nate makes me push harder. That doesn't mean I'm not in pain the whole time.

"I need water," I gasp.

"Same, but it's waiting for us back at the barn."

I give him a look of annoyance and groan in agony.

"Just try your best not to think about it," he says.

I'm trying to forget about the last three miles we have before I can sip a fresh gulp of water. My throat feels tight from the sharpness of my breathing and it burns every time I swallow my saliva due to dehydration. I look at the restaurants in front of me, attempting to take my mind off my quenching thirst. Oh, what I would give to gulp down spaghetti and meatballs. Or a slice of thick chocolate cake. The only things I've been eating for the last month are dry canned foods, protein bars, chips, and other random garbage we can find. And they aren't huge servings, just little rations of food in the morning and at night. My body is shriveling up like a burning piece of paper.

"Our break is over," Nate declares. "I'm dying for water."

I sigh and complain, "I can barely move."

"Weren't you just whining about how thirsty you are?"

"Yes, but—"

"No buts. C'mon."

I struggle getting up as Nate reaches his hand out to help me. Then I jog slowly behind him with every ounce of strength I have left.

⌐⌐

When we return to the barn, I chug down my water quickly. I feel dizzy and exhausted, but I ignore it. The more I focus on the pain, the worse it gets.

Right before we turned onto the road where our barn is, I noticed a group of three people in the distance watching us. They weren't close enough for me to depict their faces. It freaked me out, which caused me to run faster, but I didn't say anything to Nate. I didn't want the people to know I saw them. I tried my best to remain calm. They could have just been ordinary strangers on a walk. But it still rubbed me the wrong way.

"Did you see those people staring at us?" I ask Nate.

"People? Where?"

"At the corner of the road where we take our last left turn."

"Were they your parents?"

"No, I don't think so. I mean, I don't know. If it was, someone else was with them. I didn't get a good look. All I know is there were three of them, but who knows? They could've just been random people."

"No. This barn is very secluded. No one ever comes back here."

"They weren't right back here. Remember? I said they were at the corner."

"Still. It's better to be safe than sorry."

"Oh my god, you and your freaking crazy suspicions," I scoff. "Why can't you just look at life with a little bit of optimism?"

"Because that's unrealistic. And doing that is gonna get myself killed."

I begin to pace around with frustration and worry. Nate is right, but I don't want to admit it. I want to continue living in a lovely fantasy where I know I am safe and no one will go so far as to hurt me or hunt me down, but pretending can also destroy you. I keep arguing because, for some reason, it gives me a sense of power over things I know are out of my control.

"This is why I didn't wanna tell you in the first place."

The look in Nate's eyes changes. He's angrier now. Not scary angry, just angry. But I'm also not so sure. He can be hard to read at times.

"We're a team," Nate affirms, his lower lip quivering. "We stick together. Always. And we do not keep secrets. No matter what."

"I know, I'm sorry. I didn't mean—"

"No, sorry," Nate apologizes, his expressions softening. "I-I shouldn't have freaked like that. Let's just . . . be careful, I guess."

"Okay, I will."

"I need to go get some fresh air," Nate mumbles and leaves out the back.

Guilt begins to sink in. Nate still doesn't know about Trevor. It's not like I'm obligated to tell him I have a boyfriend. Am I? I don't know, but the way Nate looked at me when he said we're a team has me thinking that whenever he does find out about Trevor, it's not going to end well. Sometimes I wish people could just know things without you having to tell them. That is the case with Nate most of the time. He can read everyone else's mind but mine. I'm glad I get that privacy, though. There are some things I don't want anyone to know, and I would like to keep it that way.

I fix my eyes toward the floor of the barn. I wonder what everyone back home thinks of me. Do they remember I exist? Or was I just a speck of dust to them? Maybe they all forgot about me. It's not like anyone has been looking for me, except my parents, but that's because they're teamed up with the bad guys. Is anybody mad that I'm gone? Or scared? Or are they celebrating? Do they think I'm dead? Will I ever see any of my friends again? Or will I just stay hidden with Nate for the rest of my life?

All of a sudden, there's a rat-a-tat against the front barn door or at least what's left of it. My body shakes with fear. Did the Deal and Do find me? They must've been the ones who I saw. They must've followed us back to the barn. Am I still going to be alive twenty-four hours from now?

"Nate?" I tremble softly. "Nate, do you hear that?"

He must still be outside, so I have to answer it. I tiptoe cautiously over to the door. I lift a plank of wood to see . . . Sadie. Sadie? What the hell is she doing here? Someone must care that I'm missing; otherwise, she wouldn't be here. It's good to finally see a familiar face. I step out and look at the sky. Nate taught me how to tell time by the sun and stars. It's a little after 4:00 p.m.

"Sadie! What are you doing here?"

"There's not much time," she replies in a deep and serious tone, her light brown hair blowing around in the breeze.

"What do you mean?"

"The members of the Deal and Do Company know where you are. I overheard them making plans with your parents and Violet at the school. They're coming here to attack exactly a month from now, on the evening of December first, but you can't leave now. They've been at the school and your parents' house a lot lately, and they've also been roaming through the town every day. It's too dangerous."

"What, are you serious? Oh my god, what am I gonna do? I can't just sit here and wait." I thought I was safe out here with Nate, but now I don't know if safety will ever be an option again. It seems that every time I find a new shelter, I'm forced to flee it.

"Don't worry. Me, Trevor, Carla, Teresa, Nala have a plan. The night before the attack, you are going to leave this place as empty as you found it. If you leave on time, you should arrive at the school before sunset the next day. By that time, they won't be there anymore. They'll be on their way to the barn looking for you. Nala and Teresa have started digging a small but big enough hole for you to hide in behind the football field. There's not much progress yet, but they're doing a good job. Carla, Trevor, and I are working on a fight plan for when the Deal and Do members arrive back at home. I just want you to be safe. You are my best friend."

Fear and adrenaline swim through me after hearing this news. I hate being targeted, especially like this.

"I'm so scared, but thank you for telling me."

"It's okay . . ." Her voice trails off as a sad, distant expression appears on her face.

"Is something wrong?" I ask.

"No, I'm just worried about you. I hate to say it, but you aren't looking so good. And you're living in this broken-down pile of wood. Are you sure you don't want me to stay with you or bring back stuff from home?"

"You are so sweet, but I'm trying to stay as hidden as possible."

"Okay, are you sure?" she repeats.

"I'm sure."

"How'd you find this place anyways?" she asks while glancing behind me.

"I actually got lucky. I woke up the morning after I ran away, and I found this guy, Nate. I begged him for help, and he hesitated at first, but I convinced him, and he brought me to this barn he's been living in for three years. But the weirdest thing was I could sense there was this connection between us. Turns out, he has powers too. Isn't that so cool?"

"Wow, you did get lucky. What's his power?"

"He can read minds."

I hear footsteps from behind me. I glance back to see Nate walking toward us.

"Is that him?"

"Yeah."

"Well, I better get going now. Nala's brother is waiting in the car for me."

"Oh, can I come say hi?"

But she's gone before she can hear me.

"What the hell!" Nate begins as he approaches me. "I was looking for you everywhere. Who the fuck was that? I thought I told you not to tell anyone where we are. And I told you earlier to be careful. Why did you let her talk to you? Now who knows how much danger we could be in? She could go back and tell everyone where we are. Did you tell her about me?"

"Relax, Nate. It's not anyone bad. She's just a friend of mine. You don't need to be my Mother Gothel."

"Mother Gothel?" he questions. "Who's that?"

"You know, from the movie *Tangled*?"

"Oh, I never saw it."

"It doesn't matter. All I'm saying is, you don't need to be so overprotective. I can take care of myself."

"I am not being overprotective!"

I throw him a look.

He mocks my expression. "Now will you answer my original question? Did you tell her about me or not?"

"No," I lie. "Why would I?"

"I don't know. What did she say?"

"She said that on the night before December first, we need to leave the barn as empty as we found it."

"Why?"

"I'm getting to that, but we should probably head inside first just to be safe."

CHAPTER 18
GOOD OR EVIL

"How does she know all of this?" Nate asks after I finish telling him about the plan. We are sitting in his horse stable on a thin, torn, and dirty blanket.

"I told you. The Deal and Do has been at the school and my house a ton lately. Sadie is my neighbor and best friend. She's probably spying on them."

"Probably?"

"Oh my god. This is the same thing as earlier. Why are you so annoying to talk to?"

"Well, that's nice."

"I'm sorry, okay? There's no 'probably.' Let me start over. She *is* spying on them. Sadie would never let me down."

"Okay, if you say so."

"What is the big deal? Sadie is a very trustworthy person and would never let anyone hurt me. I know her way better than you do. Why do you not trust her?"

"I never said I didn't. All I'm saying is this is a very risky move."

"Well, how I see it is that life is all about taking risks. If you never take a risk, you'll be missing out on everything. So would you rather both of us die in this barn, or would you rather save ourselves by listening to Sadie?"

Nate rolls his eyes and gives up on arguing. "I guess the second one."

"Okay, good. Then there's nothing to worry about."

I walk out of his stable and over to mine. I sit on the ground, hugging my legs and resting my head on my knees. I stare out into the distance at the colorful, crisp autumn leaves. I review my conversation with Sadie. I wish it would've lasted longer. I still want us to be friends, and the more I can't see her, the more I feel like we're drifting apart. I wonder why Nate was so skeptical of her. Sadie is the least wavering person I know.

She's sensitive and can be unpredictable at times, but she's always there for her friends.

Maybe he could sense something in her mind that made him suspicious.

"Nate?"

"Yeah?"

"Did you see something in Sadie's mind you didn't like? Is that why you don't trust her?"

"No, I wasn't able to get a clear view, just blurred fog," Nate explains. "She ran away before I could get close enough to her. Remember, I can't read people's minds unless I'm within ten feet of them."

"Oh okay. Then never mind."

"Why'd you ask?"

"I was just curious."

"Okay. I'm gonna get myself a snack. You want anything?"

"What time is it?"

"Let me check." He takes a look outside, then says, "It's almost six."

"Okay. Yeah, you can grab me some chips or something too. That would be great."

A moment later Nate kneels down and hands me a half-empty bag of Lay's. I shove a couple of chips in my mouth.

"Thanks," I mumble while chewing.

"No problem. By the way, the plan is great. They'll never suspect us gone."

All I'm thinking is, if it weren't for Sadie, I wouldn't be alive that much longer.

CHAPTER 19
PAST VERSUS PRESENT

I open my eyes and stretch my arms up to the sky. A yawn escapes from the back of my throat as I stand and crack my back. I peek over my stable to see Nate curled up in a ball with his eyes shut tight. He looks pretty cute with his mouth just barely open. I continue watching as his lips curl into a partial smile. For a minute I wonder if he's dreaming about me.

I haven't stopped thinking about the escape plan ever since Sadie informed me earlier this month. It's such a devious scheme. I step outside and brace the cold, teeth-chattering winds. I shove my hands inside the sleeves of my sweater and clench them into fists as an attempt to warm myself up. I curl my toes inside my shoes as well, but nothing helps. I'm as cold as a frozen ice block.

Tomorrow night Nate and I will run away. If you think about it, we aren't really running away. We're just going back to where we came from. At least I am. I actually don't know where Nate used to live.

I wonder what's going to happen after tomorrow night. I can't go back to my house, and I can't come back here. I'm thinking Carla's house will probably be the best option. We'll figure it out. Sadie is great at making plans. She'll do the job. Right now I just need to take everything one step at a time.

I almost jump with excitement at the fact that I'll be able to see Trevor. I haven't seen him for more than two months. My brain flashes back to our first kiss. That night in the park. I can still feel the memory of his lips against mine. My face grows warm at the thought. And that time we cried together in Teresa's house. He was crying because he wanted me to be safe. Looking back at those moments reminds me of how easy life was just a few months ago, and I am suddenly hit with the painful weight of nostalgia. Nostalgia is a confusing feeling. It's comforting, but at times it makes me want to cry, remembering how innocent and naive I was. I thought I was going to live a great life as an ordinary high schooler with the best friends in the world and even a boyfriend on the first day of freshman year. I had it all, but was it really worth it?

Yes, Trevor reminds me of happiness and nostalgia and innocence, but he's not the only guy on my mind right now. There's also Nate. I haven't wanted to admit that because it makes me feel ashamed. I would be cheating on Trevor if I said I liked Nate. But I can't keep lying to myself. Nate is hot. His muscles are very nice and toned. Plus, his smile makes me want to melt every time it appears on that lovely face of his. And his jawline is perfect. But it's not just the looks; Nate is such a good listener. He does his best to stay patient with me and to understand me. He wants me to be safe too, doesn't he? That's why he's nervous about tomorrow. He doesn't want me to get hurt. The problem is I have two boys who want to protect me. What's going to happen when they meet each other?

And I still haven't told Nate about Trevor. The guilt has been nagging at me throughout the past month. I hate keeping things from Nate. I think it could have something to do with those strange gut feelings I've been having around him. It's almost as if the powers inside my and Nate's bodies are bonding us together even when we don't choose to. Either way, I should tell Nate before we go back to Brevard because I know how much he hates surprises. I don't want to make him uncomfortable, and I definitely don't want him getting angry with me. I haven't seen much of Nate's angry side. I think I saw a glimpse of it when I first met him, but I get the feeling he tries to hide most of those kinds of emotions from me.

"Hey," Nate says with a yawn, his voice bringing me back to reality. "You enjoying the sunrise?"

He walks up next to me. I'm leaning against an old oak tree, a bit diagonal to the back of the barn. I gaze at the sky. The sun is creating a warm ombre rainbow, purple to orange to whitish blue. "Yeah, it's nice."

Before I can control myself, I begin to tell him about Trevor. "Hey, so, Nate, there's actually—"

He quickly interrupts me. "So I was thinking, instead of spending our last day here by ourselves, maybe we could hang by the pond for a bit together. You know, it's really peaceful there. We could make it a bit of a picnic by bringing some snacks with us or whatever. I mean, if you don't want to, that's fine. I just thought maybe . . ."

"Oh," I reply, flustered and distracted. "Oh yeah, that sounds great! I would love that."

"Great! Weren't you gonna say something?"

"I . . . don't remember."

I decide now is not the time to bring up Trevor. Nate is so happy, and I don't want to crush his joy with awkwardness. I'll save that discussion for a better time, and for now, I should go enjoy our time at the pond.

"Okay," he says with hesitation in his voice. I hate playing these games with him.

He's a mind reader, for God's sake. He knows when someone is lying better than anyone.

"But if you do, just tell me."

"I will."

Nate and I are sitting on the large rock, gazing at the pond. I begin to zone out as I stare into the rippling water. A lot has happened on this rock. It was where I sat right after I received the letter from my parents. This was almost like my escape rock, where I ran to when I needed space. I spent a lot of my first nights here crying and regretting my life. There's also my growth stump, the tree stump I sat on many times, contemplating troubling thoughts and growing my mentality. Nate's arm lightly brushes against mine, sending butterflies to my stomach.

He sighs and asks, "So what are we going to do after we get to Brevard?"

"I'm not exactly sure, but I was thinking we'd stay at my friend Carla's house. She doesn't have any siblings, and her parents are really nice. They also live close to the school, so that's a plus."

"Where do you go to school?"

"Brevard High School." After a noticeable pause in our conversation, I ask, "Where'd you used to live again?"

"In this random town called Marion. It's about an hour drive from there to Brevard. We would pass through there sometimes while traveling."

"That must've been a far walk to the barn."

"It really was. I was so relieved when I found this place."

"I bet."

"It's beautiful there," Nate says, looking up at the trees. I can tell by his tone of voice that he's getting that same sad, complex nostalgia I was experiencing earlier. "I remember I would go to this park near our house all the time. When I was younger, I had a favorite swing I'd always go on. And the view of the mountains was gorgeous."

"Brevard is pretty similar. Beautiful mountain views, pretty parks . . ."

"I know. But nothing can ever compare to my hometown. That was my happy place, and whenever I think of nostalgia, I smell my old house. My mom was always making something good in the kitchen, and I could smell it from my bedroom. You know what I mean?"

"Yeah, I do. I get that same feeling, except I don't really smell anything. I guess I'm not as sentimental as you."

"Well, everybody's different."

"Thank you for helping me," I say after a minute of silence.

"What do you mean?"

"When we first met, you were all I had. I probably would've died if you didn't bring me to this barn."

"Oh c'mon. You don't need to thank me. I'm glad I helped you anyways.

If I didn't, I never would've known what an amazing person you are."

"That is literally the nicest thing you've said to me."

"Well, it's true. I've never met anyone like you."

We sit there, gazing at each other for the longest time. I laugh lightheart-edly, but don't turn away. Nate's beautiful amethyst eyes continue to entice me. My heart begins to tie itself into knots, and I feel like I can't breathe. I can barely process the fact that Nate's head is slowly inching toward me. When his lips meet mine, they feel so, so perfect. I want to keep kissing him. The greatest feeling enters my body, but it doesn't last long. Now it's replaced with guilt and shame. I quickly jolt my head back. Nate grows stiff with embarrassment and confusion.

"I'm sorry. I just—" I stop myself because I don't know what to say. I'm panicking on the inside. "I can't do this right now."

I rush back to the barn quickly, leaving Nate alone on the rock. I make it to my horse stable and curl up in the corner. I can't describe all the emotions inside me right now. Kissing Nate felt way better than it did with Trevor, if I'm being honest. But what is Trevor going to say when he finds out I cheated on him? What is Nate going to say when he finds out I kept my boyfriend a secret from him all this time? And what am I to do? I know I need to choose one side or the other, but I don't think I know how.

CHAPTER 20
CONFESSIONS

"So . . . do you wanna talk about it?" Nate awkwardly asks. "You know, since you were avoiding me yesterday?"

I turn away from him. A sharp blast of wind hits my face, almost like ice-cold nails. The weather is miserable today—cloudy, windy, and freezing. It's not like the barn provides much warmth either. Besides, I came outside as soon as I woke up this morning, attempting to escape Nate's presence. Avoiding him is almost a way for me to ignore my feelings.

"There's nothing to talk about," I reply in a harsh tone.

"Oh really? So then why were you so angry afterwards?"

"Why are you being so pushy? Maybe I just wasn't ready."

"I'm not trying to be pushy. I just want to understand what's going on here." Nate continues when I don't respond. "I might not be able to read your mind, but I sure as hell can read body language. I know you might be uncomfortable talking about it, or you might be afraid I'll get upset, but I'm already upset. There's no point in hiding any longer. It'll just make you feel worse."

"Okay, fine. Yes, I have a boyfriend. And I guess I should've told you this sooner, before something happened between us, but I don't know. I didn't really think I needed to. But also, I was planning to tell you. Yesterday morning, remember? I start saying something. Then you were in such a good mood, and I didn't wanna ruin that. I felt like telling you about him would make things more awkward between us. But now things already are awkward between us, so good for me I guess."

"Things don't need to be awkward unless we make it that way. We don't have to talk about this again. And we can pretend none of this ever happened and move on as friends. I'm just glad you told me."

"Okay. Thank you," I say, relief rushing through me.

I'm shocked at the way Nate handled that with such maturity. This whole time I was scared he would get angry or upset, but he was so empathetic and forgiving. And how he said we can move on as friends instead of being petty and giving me the silent treatment. Nate's reaction to this situation makes me feel more comfortable around him than I did before.

"Okay, well, we should probably get our stuff together for later," Nate says, changing the subject. "We gotta make this place look abandoned again."

I find some sort of motivation inside me and stand up off the tree stump. I walk back inside the barn and over to the empty chip bags and snack wrappers in the corner.

As I crouch down to pick up the waste, I sit there for a minute, beginning to zone out. Memories from home are cycling through my brain. I try to recall what the drama was at school before I left. Before I read the school newspaper that changed my life. Oh, I remember. Spencer hit me because he thought I was the one to blame for Sadie's breakup with him. So stupid. The red mark is gone, but I still remember the pain like it was yesterday. Scars, visible or invisible, are a mark of your strength, and you shouldn't feel ashamed of them. It only reveals how much you've gone through.

"Whatcha thinking?" Nate questions, kneeling down beside me.

"It doesn't matter."

"Well, I wanna hear it anyways."

I hesitate. Nate doesn't know too much about what my life was like before I met him. Only that Sadie and I have been friends for a long time and that I go to Brevard High School. He also knows a little bit about my family situation, but telling him about Spencer will make me look weaker.

But for some weird reason, my gut attests. What is it with my gut feelings and Nate? Is it really our powers? Do they connect us somehow? Either way, I should trust my gut. It got me away from the danger back at home. It also brought Nate and me together, and although things aren't the same between us now, I still think we're supposed to be with each other. As friends.

"I guess I can tell you. It's a long story, though."

"That's fine. You can tell me while we clean this stuff up. We do need something to entertain us."

"Okay," I start, "so Sadie's parents are divorced. They have been for a really long time. Her mom has a boyfriend now, and Sadie hasn't been taking it very well. I didn't know that, so when she was avoiding everyone and acting a little standoffish, I thought she had a problem with me or I did something wrong. I was very suspicious of it, and at lunch one day, she was late again, and I was talking about her with some of my friends, including her boyfriend, Spencer. Well, her ex-boyfriend now. I asked if she told him anything, and it turns out that Sadie heard us talking about her."

"Oh god. I see where this is going."

"Yeah, so she asked Spencer what he was saying, and he said nothing, and then I popped off on her about . . . actually, I don't really know why I was that mad, but it's over now. So then she told us about her mom's new boyfriend, and she got mad at us and everything. It was really embarrassing because a bunch of other students were looking. Later that day at school, Spencer found me in the hallway and was super pissed because somehow it was my fault that they broke up, and then he hit me in the face. Even though it didn't leave a bruise, I felt this terrible weight in my chest afterwards. It did not feel good."

"What the hell?" Nate exclaims. "He actually hit you? That's literal abuse."

"Yeah, I know. It was scary. We told the principal and he got in trouble, but still, like, who does that? It wasn't even my fault."

"I know it wasn't," Nate says, looking into my eyes with deep compassion. The comfort begins to turn into awkward nerves again. The feelings go away when Nate continues. "What did you do? Like after he hit you?"

I laugh uncomfortably before explaining, "I obviously cried because it hurt really bad. I just sat there in the hallway sobbing until my friend

Teresa came by and helped me. It was kinda embarrassing."

"You've got a lot of friends."

"Not that many," Judging by the look on his face, I add, "Trust me. I'm not popular."

"Hah, okay. Anyways, that whole situation sounds terrible. I'm so sorry you had to go through something like that."

"Yeah. It was fine, though. And Sadie and I, as you can tell, have made up, and we're great friends again."

"What about that Spencer guy?"

"Oh, I'm never talking to him again."

"I know I wouldn't."

We share a moment of laughter until it fades into silence once again.

"Thank you," I say.

"For what?"

"For everything."

"Oh, c'mon. You keep saying that."

"Because . . . it's true."

I raise my expression to a genuine smile. It's so nice to have a guy like Nate who I can vent to about my friend problems because he's not on any side. He always understands what I'm going through, and I find reassurance in that. I notice that Nate's smile disappears, and his face grows stiff.

"What is it?"

"I meant to tell you earlier, but there's something I need to show you. It's important."

"Okay?" I hesitate. "Is it bad?"

"It's not that bad. It's just something you need to see."

CHAPTER 21
HISTORY OF THE ENEMIES

I look at Nate with confusion. What is he about to show me? Should I be scared or excited? With curiosity and uncertainty, I follow him outside and down a narrow path I somehow never noticed before. It's to the left of the barn, and the pond is to the right. We start on the path, the sound of footsteps crunching on leaves taking over. Dark green trees begin to cave around us.

"What's back here?"

"You'll see."

I try to think of what could possibly be back here, but my brain is fogged with memories of Trevor. I keep trying to tell myself I'm not betraying him. That Nate is only protecting me out here while he waits back home for me. And I've already made it clear with Nate that we're only friends. But what if Trevor has given up on me? What if he's forgotten about me and is with a new girl now? No, I tell myself, he's part of Sadie's runaway escape plan. He still cares about me.

"Here we are," Nate declares.

On the ground ahead of me is a large cream-colored paper. I step closer and kneel down. I brush away the dirt and leaves covering the mysterious artifact. Part of me is scared to touch whatever this is, but I do it anyway. All sorts of dates and years fill the paper. I think it's a timeline. When Nate said he had something to show me, I'm not sure what I was expecting. But it definitely wasn't this.

"What is this?"

"This . . . is a timeline of the Deal and Do Company."

Ready to investigate the history behind my enemies, I inch closer.

Timeline of the Deal and Do Company (updated 9/21/2014)

1960: The Deal and Do Company was established in Worcester, Massachusetts by Billy Smith, a scientific mastermind, and his companion, Frank Macon. Its name was created by Frank when he said, "We make deals with people to do great things."

1963: After making a deal with the local robotics club, Billy and Frank created their first experiment, the Watching Bird, a robotic bird with built-in cameras. Its experimental name was Project Vigilantes Avem, which, in Latin, translates to Project Watching Bird.

1964: Project Vigilantes Avem was found flying across one of the beaches of Massachusetts. A group of children found it and attempted to take it home with them. The scientists were fed up with these series of events and went into hiding.

1971: Billy died of pneumonia at age 33 and the company shut down.

1997: The company was reunited through Frank and Billy's sons, Raymond Macon and Daniel Smith, taking over.

1998: Raymond and Daniel started experimenting with plants, trying to help the environment.

1999: The two sons won an award for their amazing work.

2001: The sons began to grow bored with plants and were eager to take over the world. They believed they could do so if they created human experiments and injected special powers into younglings.

2002: Stephanie and Dave Gresham joined the company as Raymond and Daniel's lead assistants. Raymond and Daniel searched for other scientific experts. In response to the search, they gained four new members, who prefer to stay anonymous.

2003: The Deal and Do went through with their ambitious idea. They gathered a group of orphans and abandoned kids. They were only successful in keeping two of the kids. They are known today as Calypso Gresham and Nathaniel Thompson, who were ages three and five at the time. Their experimental names are Project Coalipo and Project Animus Concertator. Animus Concertator translates to Mind Struggler in Latin. Coalipo has no specific meaning to it and is the first project name used by The Deal and Do that isn't Latin. Daniel said to him it was a word of mystery, just like this experiment of theirs. The company did succeed in giving the children powers, but they did not succeed in their ultimate goal: keeping the children to themselves so they could rule over.

2003: Project Animus Concertator fled the Deal and Do headquarters and was adopted by a young couple (names unknown).

2004: Stephanie and Dave adopted Calypso, so she could still be in the eyes of the company without the girl ever finding out.

2007: Gregory Samson joined the company.

2008: Diana Hoffman, Lily Lockhorn, and Steven joined the company.

2011: Jonah and A. L. Walters joined the company.

2012: Levi Anderson joined the company.

July 17 2014: Sally joined the company.

September 19 2014: Project Coalipo fled her home and her current whereabouts are unknown.

In a tiny font at the very bottom, it says,

The Deal and Do's main goal: to steal the two power projects' gifts. How do they achieve this goal?

They create a complementary liquid that is the polar opposite of the chemicals inside the power projects and pour it down the power projects' throats after they are put to sleep. Then they cut a hole in the chests of the power projects and wait for all the blood to drain.

Then the only thing that's left is the chemicals, which the Deal and Do leaders pour into a tube, place in the fridge for two weeks, then drink. After that, the power is planted in the minds and bodies of the Deal and Do leaders.

A dreadful terror makes my heart drop. I glance over at Nate, expecting him to say something. Like, first of all, how he came across this timeline in the first place. But he collapses to the ground. His face and limbs begin to shake vigorously as if he's going through a trance. I rush over to him and bend down by his side. I hold his trembling body in my arms as I try to wake him up. I shout his name, but can barely hear myself over the heavy panic. I don't know what is happening or how to stop it. I do everything I can to try and help, but he's only getting worse.

* * *

Calypso looks sick to her stomach. I'm about to tell her how crazy it is that we got our powers from the Deal and Do. We both thought we earned them otherwise, and that Raymond and Daniel only wanted them to gain more control. It never occurred to me that this was all some sort of experiment made by the evil masterminds themselves.

But I am suddenly stricken with the most throbbing and heavy headache. It's so heavy I am knocked to the ground. A blinding white light shields my vision. Then at the blink of an eye, a memory of a little boy appears in my mind. He looks just like me—dark hair, brown skin, thick lips, and sharp eyebrows. Only he's smaller. Why am I seeing an image of my younger self? What is this supposed to mean?

Little me looks up with fear in his eyes. The kids around me are screaming and crying. By the looks of it, I'm in an adoption center. A large man attacks the women who are helping the kids escape. But little me doesn't even try to run. The two men yank me by my scrawny arms. I attempt a weak kick, but it's useless.

Time speeds up in the vision. Now I'm in the back of a van with a younger girl. I knew her from the adoption center. I have no memory of anything I'm seeing, but now that I'm reliving it, parts are coming back to me. This girl doesn't cry. She just looks at me with a gaping mouth, drool oozing out the one side. Her mystical gray eyes and wispy dark hairs reveal who she is—Young Calypso.

Time speeds up again. I watch as little me screams at the four men standing by. I look so small and vulnerable with only a diaper on as I lie on the table in a bright white room.

"Daniel! Hurry the hell up! This kid is getting feisty with us!" one of the men shouts.

"I'm trying!"

Daniel hands another man a massive syringe filled with bright purple serum, the same color as my eyes. He jams it into my neck before my body goes limp.

Fast-forward to me in a different room on an air mattress. This room is all dark except for a faint blue light reflecting off the machines in the corner. The atmosphere is unpleasant, especially with the gray brick wall and cement flooring around me. My body is shaking, and I have three different tubes attached to my arm.

A new image now cuts in. I'm tearing the tubes painfully out of my arm. Little me squirms and wails in agony, but I manage to be successful in the end. Once I'm free I start limping across the building until I am outside.

Fast-forward to me shivering and crying on the edge of a sidewalk curb. A young couple appears—Joel and Harper.

"Hey, kid," Joel says slowly while kneeling down to meet my height. "Where are your parents?"

"W-What parents?" I ask, my lips trembling.

Joel and Harper share a look of concern.

"You know, your mommy and daddy. Are they not with you?"

"N-No."

"Here, why don't you come with us? We've got a nice, warm home, and Harper can make you a yummy plate of chocolate chip cookies."

"C-C-Cookies?"

"Yes, I'm sure you'll love them," Harper adds.

"Her food is truly the best," Joel says.

The visions all fade away as my mind goes blank. It takes a minute for me to return to reality. Calypso is holding me tight in her arms. I notice tears are forming at the edges of her eyes.

"Oh my god, Nate! Nate, are you okay?" she bursts out in panic.

"I-I don't know. I just . . . saw my past."

"What? What do you mean?"

"I don't think it was just that we were too young to remember what happened to us," I explain. "I think Raymond and Daniel wiped our memory so that we wouldn't know our powers came from them and we wouldn't know we were taken from the same adoption center."

"What the hell? The same adoption center, are you for real? That's insane. What did you see?"

"I'll tell you everything. Just give me a minute."

* * *

"I saw a bunch of stuff," Nate begins. I can tell he's still stunned by what just happened. My state of shock is continuing, and I wasn't even the one having the visions. I can't imagine what he is feeling. "First, I saw five-year-old me in the adoption center. And like I said, we were both at the same one. We knew each other as little kids."

"That's so . . . weird. But wait. That makes so much sense. Because I've always felt this weird connection between us, probably from our powers, but also somewhere in the back of my brain, I knew we had met before. I just couldn't remember. And now that I'm thinking about it, I have no memories of my childhood until I was like five. I never thought anything of it. I just thought I was too young."

"Yeah, I mean age was definitely a part of it, but from what I saw, I know they drugged us a ton. And even though we were so young, those events were so intense, we should've at least remembered the feeling."

"Yeah, that's true. What else happened?"

"Well, then I saw Raymond and Daniel. They beat up the ladies at the foster home and took me. It was so weird. These visions made it feel like I was watching this happen to somebody else. But it was all me. Just . . . a different version."

"I know. This completely changes everything," I say. "The fact that the Deal and Do aren't just after some silly powers for fun, they're after us. They are the ones who created our abilities."

"No, I know. It makes me sick to think about. So yeah, then I saw both of us in the back of a van. Next thing I knew, I was on a table having a needle jammed into my neck. They were giving me my powers. I also saw myself attached to all these different IVs and tubes because the Deal and Do was drugging me with a bunch of shit I didn't need. And I'm guessing one of those was distorting my memory so that all I would remember was being at an adoption center, then all of a sudden being with Harper and Joel."

Nate's eyes flicker away from me to the ground. His eyes begin to water. He sucks in his lower lip, trying to fight off the tears.

"I always knew there were cruel people out there." Nate's voice shakes. "But why do they have to be coming after us?"

"I don't know."

Now we're both crying. I wrap my arms around Nate, and he envelops me in a hug. A long, emotional hug. I'm sad and scared, but at least my heart is warm.

At last, Nate lets go and wipes away his tears.

"We should be getting back to the barn," he says.

"Yeah, I guess we should."

Our walk back is silent until the last minute when Nate continues. "I can't believe I had to go through all that at such a young age. And you too. I mean, you were even younger. And you've never been free. All these years and you were still living with the Deal and Do. I fled Raymond and Daniel. I saw it. I yanked those IVs out of my arm and ran. Then Joel and

Harper found me and took me in. It was such a weird sight. Seeing my parents again in a vision. And I was shaking so badly from the drugs. This all feels so unreal."

"Yep," I say, biting dry skin off my lip. "I still can't believe I thought of Stephanie and Dave as my mom and dad. It was all an act. I know we already knew that, but I still can't get over it. They aren't just working for the Deal and Do. They're literally their right-hand men."

"And you might never get over it. But that's okay."

I nod and smile at Nate, but on the inside, I'm thinking, How is any of this okay?

"Oh, I forgot to give this to you also," Nate mentions, handing me a folded piece of paper. "It came with the timeline."

"What is it?"

"I don't know. Some sort of note. I didn't read it. I just saw your name was on it."

For Calypso

Don't give your trust to those who will only abuse it.

"What the hell?" I mutter under my breath. "Look at this."

I show Nate the message. He looks up and asks, "Who's it from?"

"I'm not sure. It looks familiar, though. I'm not good with remembering handwriting or stuff like that, so I don't know."

"Do you think it's Sadie's?"

"Could be. I mean, it looks familiar. It probably is. Who else would send a timeline of the Deal and Do with this note? She's the one who's been spying on them and everything, and she wants us to be safe."

"True. So it probably is her."

I fold the paper back up and crumple it in my pocket. At least the card can be a temporary distraction from the eeriness of the timeline, although I don't think I'm ever going to forget about that. Some things are implanted in your mind forever, whether you wish for them to be there or not.

CHAPTER 22
ALMOST CAUGHT

Outside the barn, the dark navy sky is filled with stars twinkling next to the almost full moon. I take a deep breath. There's not much time left before we have to go. The thought of walking all the way back to where I've been missing from for two months fills me with exhaustion. I have missed so many things at school. Not like those are important. I think my life as a normal teenager is over now. No normal teenager hides in a barn with a stranger for survival.

To avoid thinking about the timeline, I ponder over my friends. Their life has been moving on without me. Things will have changed. I, for one, have definitely changed. What if they don't like me anymore? What if I come back and all my friends have ditched me? At least I can always count on Sadie to be there for me. Hell, if it weren't for her, I would be left to suffer the consequences of the Deal and Do finding Nate and me here tomorrow night.

"It's almost nine," Nate says, halting my train of thought. "We should probably get going now."

"Okay," I say with a grunt as I stand up from the floor.

I grab the plastic bag from my stable. Earlier, I put all our belongings in there, which only consists of our water bottles and a couple of snacks to give us energy on our journey home. A minute later, Nate and I head out the front of the barn and onto the gravel pathway. The straps of the plastic bag are already chafing the inside of my elbow, but I do my best to ignore it. We stop for a second, and I glance back at the barn one last time. I'm glad to be leaving this place, but I'm also afraid of what is ahead.

"You ready?"

I sigh. "Yeah, I think so."

"Okay, let's go."

It must be close to 9:30 p.m. when Nate starts looking around confused, turning in circles and peering in every direction. I continue to follow him, although I'm not sure if I should. He stomps his foot on the ground in annoyance. "You know where we are? 'Cause I feel so fucking lost."

"I don't know. I thought you said you remembered how to get there."

"I said I'm pretty sure I knew because me and my family used to pass through downtown Brevard a lot when traveling. It's been a while though. You were the one who walked from there to the barn. Shouldn't you know?"

"I'm not good with directions. Aren't you supposed to be Mr. Survival Guy? Shouldn't you have a map in your brain or something?"

"Ha ha. So funny," he says with monotonous sarcasm.

I scoff at Nate, then I take a minute to focus on the scenery around me. I'm facing a tree that looks oddly familiar. I don't know what it is, but I feel like I've stood in this exact spot before. It's literally just a tree. Nothing special. I begin to investigate the branches. Then it hits me.

"Oh my god. This is where I first met you!" I exclaim. Even though it was only a couple of months ago, it feels like it's been forever.

"Oh, yeah. I see it now. I think I know where we are."

"I mean, over there was technically where I met you, but this is the tree I fell asleep under the night before."

"You're right. See, maybe you're not so bad with directions after all."

"Well, this isn't really a map. I just remembered what the tree looked like. More like a visual landmark."

Nate nods before asking, "Was it comfy?" after noticing the funny look on my face, he breaks down his question. "When you slept here, was it comfortable?"

"Nate, it's a tree. But yeah, I guess it was fine."

"I'll sleep on this side, and you can sleep on the other. Okay?"

"Okay, I'm gonna have a quick sip of water if you want some. But I promise, this time, I—"

I stop talking when Nate's head pops up abruptly.

"What?"

"You hear that?"

"Hear wha—"

Nate aggressively shushes me. He's wearing a great look of fear in his eyes, which only scares me more. But I know talking won't make this any better. The only solution is to stay quiet and hidden behind the tree with Nate. I watch as two men in business suits appear. They're far away, so I can't quite see their faces, but they're still close enough for me to see the outline of their bodies. Like silhouettes in suits. One is short and chunky, and the other is tall and muscular. They have such prominent body features, almost like cartoon characters. Raymond Macon and Daniel Smith—the owners of the Deal and Do Company. The men who want to chop open our chests, drain all our blood, and take our powers. My heart is pounding so hard against my body I can feel it in the back of my throat. I feel as if I'm going to explode. I try to calm myself down, but I don't know how.

I chew the nerves out onto my right cheek as they mumble words I can't understand. "What are they thinking?" I mutter to Nate.

"I don't know. Shh!"

The men now face our direction.

"Who's there?" Daniel, the shorter one, shouts.

We quietly inch farther behind us until Nate's back hits a fence. They must've heard it because Raymond hisses, "I know you're there. Just come out, and we'll leave you alone. We can even have a nice chat if you want."

I point behind the fence, telling Nate we need to get to the other side. He jumps over it like it's part of his everyday routine. I try to jump over as well, but turns out, I'm not tall enough. The only option is for me to crawl under. I throw the plastic bag to the other side then get down on my hands and knees. Attempting to crawl under the small space between the fence and the ground is definitely a struggle. On a normal day, I would just give up. This feels impossible, but I have no choice. I try my best not to grunt or squeal in pain as the bottom of the fence digs into my spine. Raymond and Daniel continue shouting up at us, but I can't hear what they're saying. All I can tell is they're getting closer to where we are.

"C'mon," Nate whispers anxiously.

"I'm trying."

Mud collects in my mouth. A bitter earthy taste settles on my tongue. I have no time to spit it out. I just have to make sure not to swallow. I want to gag. I want to gag and throw up so badly. But I can't. I need to ignore the pain. I need to forget about the negatives. I try to think about Sadie and Trevor and all my friends back at home. I try to imagine them cheering me on, telling me I'm strong and I can do anything I set my mind to. If I can't make it through this fence, we're stuck here with our murderous enemies. I have no choice. I need to push through.

I finally make it to the other side. Nate helps me up, and we sprint further away. I spit out the mud once we're a couple of steps down the sidewalk. We run for a few more minutes until we're sure they've lost us. My feet ache, and my arm hurts from carrying the heavy plastic bag. A large scratch on my back burns and itches in pain. My fingers graze the gash near my spine, causing it to sting a bit. The only thing I can do for now is ignore the scrapes and bruises and hope they heal quickly.

"That was close," I gasp quickly.

"I know," Nate says while panting. "It could've been a lot worse."

"Yeah. I'm just glad they didn't catch us."

"That's why we ran every morning."

"And it was worth it."

"We should probably stop here," Nate says. "We need to get enough rest for tomorrow."

"Good idea."

I sigh with relief and wipe the mud off myself as best as I can. Then I crouch down beside Nate on the small patch of grass. I catch a glimpse of the sidewalk and quiet street next to us before I close my eyes and do my best to fall asleep.

CHAPTER 23
NOTE IN THE RIVER

"Hey. You awake?" Nate asks.

"Yep. I've been up all night."

"Yeah. I didn't sleep great either."

I stretch my arms wide and jump to my feet. The sun is just barely peeking above the horizon. I'm in even worse shape than yesterday. My arms are covered with scrapes and bruises, and my clothing is damp from the mud. My dirty white Converse are beat up and torn, and my socks have holes in them as well. My strength is draining. I rub my eyes and reach into the plastic bag before handing it to Nate. I take a small sip of my water and save the rest, even though I need more. My mouth is drier than a desert and the mud situation last night didn't help. There's only a little more than half a bottle left. I don't know how long it'll last. And by the looks of it, I doubt rain is going to pour down anytime soon.

"I don't have much water left. Do you?" I ask Nate.

He searches the bag. "Only as much as you."

I groan in response as he hands me half of a granola bar and eats the other half. I munch on my small breakfast and look back the way we came from. My mind flashes back to me crying in the school hallway after getting hit by Spencer. What a child I was in comparison to now. Scared Calypso is no more. Courageous Calypso has taken the lead. There's still a part of her that's there. You never fully change in life; you just grow.

I feel a light breeze run through my hair. It's almost like a reassurance that I am strong.

"Time to go," Nate declares.

Although I feel like crap, I stride alongside Nate with my head held high.

⌒

Around 11:00 a.m. the line of trees ends, and I recognize the entrance to the neighborhood ahead. Trevor's neighborhood. I've only been to his house twice. Once for a Halloween party last year and once in third grade for his birthday party.

"We're close," I tell Nate.

"How close?"

"Probably about an hour and a half or so if we keep walking at this pace."

Nate nods, and we continue strolling beside the street. I let my mind drift off and begin to think about the eighth-grade Halloween party at Trevor's house. Sadie, Spencer, and I were there. The four of us dressed up as a family of vampires. We trick-or-treated some, ate candy, watched scary movies, and stayed up past 2:00 a.m.

Spencer and Trevor were creeping us out with strange ghost stories. Sadie decided to pull a hilarious prank on the neighbors. They were so angry at us. It was one of those stupid teenager moments but also a night full of fun memories. Back then, it felt like nothing mattered and I wasn't constantly worrying about whether or not I'd still be alive the next day.

As I'm thinking about this, a really bad migraine suddenly overtakes me. I'm not being dramatic. The throbbing is terrible. I ignore it and continue walking. But I only get ahead by a few more steps before I feel light-headed and dizzy.

"Cal?" Nate's voice swirls.

I try taking deep breaths. I'm fine. Why wouldn't I be fine? But on the inside, I know I need to sit down. I know my body is draining. My vision blurs, and a dingy yellow tint takes over. I know this feeling. I'm about to pass out. I almost passed out once in seventh grade. I was dehydrated and not eating enough. I'm getting the exact same feeling as I did then.

"Na . . ." My voice trails off.

I see a patch of green, which I'm assuming is grass, and I try to make it there. I need to sit down. But halfway there, I collapse.

⌣

"Cal! Cal? Can you hear me? Please say you can hear me."

"Yeah, I'm here." My voice comes out wobbly and breathy.

Nate is on the ground, kneeling over me. I feel the grass beneath me. I somehow made it here, or Nate carried me over. I'm assuming it's the last scenario. I probably look so weak right now. But that's not what I should be concerned about. Nate starts to pour water into my mouth.

I take the bottle from him and mumble, "I'm capable of doing things myself."

Nate laughs wryly at my comment. I swallow the lukewarm water, wishing there was more. Only three more sips before the bottle is basically empty. There's enough for one small sip left.

"You can have mine if you need it," Nate offers.

"No, I'm fine."

I can't take any more of this lying down business. I feel tiny and powerless. I stand up, a little too quickly, causing the dizziness to return.

"Easy," Nate cautions.

"I'm fine. Just give me a second."

The dizziness went away, but who knows how much longer I'll be able to walk. I understand why I passed out. I haven't slept or eaten great recently, which I'm still not used to. Plus, I had to unexpectedly run away from Raymond and Daniel last night. And it doesn't help that we have to walk so many miles back to Brevard High School.

"I'm gonna take a break for a sec."

"Okay, sure. I'll be here," Nate reassures.

I walk slowly behind the trees across from Trevor's neighborhood. Good thing he's at school right now. His house is toward the front of the neighborhood, and it would have been so embarrassing if he had seen me pass out.

I'm walking on a small pathway covered in leaves and pine straw. Soon, I make it to a trickling ribbon of water. I gaze at my reflection. My dark, tangled locks have definitely grown over the past couple of months. It's been awhile since my hair has met a brush. I have two noticeable scratches on my face. One on my right cheek and another near my eyebrow. I also have an ugly bruise on my chin. No idea when or how I got those. But somehow, through the filthy scars and tired eyes, I see beauty and strength.

My gaze switches its focus to the actual water. There isn't much of it, but it slowly starts to dawn on me that I've been here before. This is the same creek I threw my phone into before I ran away. We aren't far from the place I typed my last text to Trevor.

I catch something out of the corner of my eye. I look in that direction to see a phone—my phone. I bend down, reach my hand into the cold water, and pick it up. I'm expecting the screen to stay black, but it flickers on. That's weird. If my phone has been in this creek for two months now, shouldn't it be broken? I type in my password; lucky I remember it. It opens to the Notes app. A new note is shown on my screen that was written today, just a few hours ago. This doesn't make any sense. How is my phone still working, and why is there a new note on here? Who found my phone, and how?

Be wary of who you trust.

The lines have blurred between good and evil.

-V

This note freaks me out. The lines have blurred between good and evil. What does that mean? And I have no clue who it's from. V . . . who is that? I mentally count down all my friends' names, but none of them start with V. I decide not to worry about it. It's probably something from Sadie but written in code so no one knows she's helping me.

Now that I'm thinking about it, that would actually make sense. When we were younger, Sadie and I used to play imaginary princess games. I was Queen Ruby, and she was Princess Vanessa. So her code name could be V for Vanessa. She must be reminding me that Raymond and Daniel are dangerous men and they can easily deceive others.

I return my phone into the creek and trot back down the pathway. I find Nate sitting in the exact spot I left him.

"You good?" he questions.

"Yeah. I'm ready to go now."

"Okay. Also, the plastic bag tore apart, so I'm gonna have to leave it here. All that's left is my water bottle anyways, and I'll just carry it."

"Yeah, that's fine. Let's go."

"Okay."

We head back down the street, continuing our trip. My feet are still numb with pain and my energy is lacking, but I just continue the rhythm of putting one foot in front of the other. It's all I can do to not give up.

CHAPTER 24
AN UNEXPECTED TURN OF EVENTS

"Finally, we're here," I say, sighing with relief.

We are standing in front of the school's main entrance. The sun has already set, but the sky isn't fully dark. The smallest rays of sun are just barely peeking above the horizon. It feels like forever ago since I walked through these doors, but everything still looks the same. The same brick red walls, the same large parking lot, the same black doors through which we enter the building. It's all the same, except for the fact that it's empty. Not fully because a couple cars are sitting in the lot, and my friends have to be inside somewhere. It just feels weird. I've never stood in front of my high school when it was this deserted. I never had any extracurriculars or sports that made me stay here when school was over. I always walked straight home.

"Should we go inside?" Nate asks.

I'm asking myself the same thing, but I don't say that because I don't want him to think I'm doubting myself. I really don't know what I'm doing, though. All Sadie told me was to come to the school before sundown on December first. I've done that, but now what?

"It might be locked," I say while pulling the door handle, surprised it actually opens.

Nate looks at me, perplexed, and I shrug. I figured my friends went through one of the more secretive doors, but somehow they were able to get in this way. I'll just ask them later.

I whisper through the blue darkness, "This way. Follow my voice."

Soon, I feel Nate's arm brush against the back of my shoulder.

"Let's do this." I grin with ambition and enter the cafeteria.

There's a light shining bright in the corner of the large, vast room, which makes it easier to see. We tiptoe all the way to the other side and into the main hallway. Then we turn right. In the third room over, there's a light on, and I hear murmuring voices behind the shadows.

"That must be them," I quietly cheer as we continue but at faster speed.

When we approach the door, I notice the voices are mysterious and unfamiliar. They don't sound like Trevor or anyone I know. The strange voices are low and shrill. It's obvious my friends aren't in this room, but I still let my curiosity get the best of me.

"That doesn't sound like them," Nate says.

I motion for him to be quiet and peek through the small window. The people I see inside shock me greatly. I feel my heart sink to my stomach as a wave of fear and doom wash over me. Sitting on black plastic chairs are my parents, Raymond, Daniel, and a few more people—one of them being Sadie. Anger begins to boil inside of me as I realize my enemies have captured her.

"Oh my god, Sadie's in there," I gasp. "We need to help her."

Nate doesn't reply, making me feel a bit uptight.

"What's wrong?"

He flips his gaze to his feet but keeps quiet. Why is he not answering me?

"Okay, whatever. I'm going in to save my friend. I know she'd do the same for me."

I begin to take a step forward, but Nate grabs my arm.

"Cal"—his soft voice cracks—"she's not been captured . . . She's with them."

"What?"

It takes me a minute to process his words. She's not been captured . . . She's with them. She's with them. She is with them. She is a part of the Deal and Do. She's on their side. But how? None of this makes sense. And how does Nate know in the first place? Oh wait. He's close enough to read her mind. Now that I look again, I notice her sitting in unison with the team, right next to Raymond. If she were captured, she would be tied up in the corner, or she wouldn't be a part of this meeting at all.

"Are you sure?" I question, although I already know the answer.

He nods with a sympathetic look in his eyes.

But how? How could my sleepover buddy, sister by friendship, and best friend for life suddenly turn into my enemy? I feel as if I've been stabbed in the gut. I'm confused and angry at the same time. I want to stomp in there and scream at her, but I'd be risking my life at the hands of the Deal and Do. Sadie, the most loyal, helpful, and amazing friend I've ever had, turns out to be a backstabbing and betraying liar. I thought we were being saved, but this whole time we were being led into the biggest trap ever. I'm such an idiot. I never saw it coming.

How could she? It's impossible. But now that I'm thinking about it, was it really that hard to notice Sadie was hiding something? I think all the way back to the first day of school and how she disappeared while I was talking to Trevor, how she was always late to classes and lunch, how she never talked to me, how she was always "busy with dance." When I asked her what she was hiding, she lied to me and said it was an issue with her parents. This was the true secret.

When we talked at the barn, she was asking all these questions about Nate, and I was dumb enough to tell her about his powers. No wonder she left in such a hurry when he came into sight. She knew he could see right through her. I should've listened to Nate when he seemed suspicious of her, but I didn't. I was so sure I could trust Sadie.

Suddenly, I'm stuck with a question that has no answer. Who left me the mysterious note in the river, and who left that timeline with the warning about trust? Who was V?

I'm so lost in thought. I don't even notice the Deal and Do gang leaving the room, not until Sadie is standing right in front of me. Since when has she been this intimidating? She was always so sweet and gentle. I am at a loss for words.

All I can manage to say in a pitiful voice is, "How could you?"

She begins to laugh this hideous cackle. I'm starting to question if this is the real Sadie. She sounds and looks so different. Everything about her has darkened, including her clothing and hair.

"I don't know why we even became friends in the first place," she says in a belittling tone. "You're so selfish and stupid, always thinking about yourself. Never about how I was feeling."

"What? I asked you how you were doing all the time. About your family and everything. You're the one who was keeping secrets. And even so, this is going way too far."

"Nothing is too far if success is on the other side."

I want to cry. I can feel my eyes burning, but I hold back the tears with all the strength I have. Crying will only make me look and feel more stupid. I fight the urge to bite my cheek. I need to stay strong and stand my ground.

"Are you serious? How can you do this? How can you not feel at least an ounce of guilt?"

"Guilt? A true hero always feels confident about their decisions. They know what they're doing is right. That's exactly why they're a hero."

"You were and never will be a hero."

"And why is that?"

"Because a real hero would do anything to help their friends. A real hero is always loyal and a role model. A villain is a cunning, evil backstabber."

"Okay, could we all just—" Raymond starts.

"This is Raymond, by the way," Sadie introduces with a strange tone in her already-strange, new voice. It's as if she's trying to make us jealous of this new group she's a part of, which is the pettiest thing ever.

Raymond's tall and threatening persona reminds me of a serial killer, like he would kill a ton of people and still not be affected by it. He is dressed in a bulky black suit, similar to what he was wearing in the newspaper photo. The two leaders are standing shoulder to shoulder. I notice my parents standing behind the two men. I'm also angry at them but decide not to acknowledge their presence. Along with them are three others. A man with jet-black hair and a narrow face. A lady with intense brown curls and thin, dark lips. And a young man, probably in his late twenties, with dirty blond hair, light blue eyes, and a very round face.

"Please, no interruptions, Sally." Raymond continues eloquently. "Thank you. Now that we have what we need, we have nothing to worry about."

Sally? What a strange nickname. My mind is suddenly reminded of the timeline in the forest. July 17 2014: Sally joined the company. Sally isn't just a random member of the Deal and Do. Sally is Sadie. The dizziness I felt earlier begins to kick in, but I pretend it's not there. How did I not notice at the time? I was blindly putting my trust in Sadie without even thinking about the possibility she could be fooling us.

"Yeah, you do," Nate says.

"And what might that be?"

"We have something you don't—powers."

"Wait a minute," Daniel realizes. "Is that AC? Our other project. Weren't you dead?"

AC? What does that mean? My mind once again flickers back to the timeline. The initials of Nate's "project name." AC. Animus Concertator.

"Do I look dead?"

"Son of a—"

"I told you," Sadie says with a proud smirk.

At that moment I snap and watch everything but my and Nate's bodies freeze. Wait a minute, shouldn't Nate be frozen as well? Why is he still moving? Are my powers not working? They worked on everyone else.

"What's happening?" I ask in a whisper, even though there's no need to keep quiet. Everyone and everything in the world is temporarily paused. Except for us.

"I think I might know," Nate says.

"What do you mean?"

"If I can't read your mind because of your powers, then—"

I finish his sentence. "I can't make you freeze." A small laugh escapes my throat due to all the emotions swimming through me. "God, this just keeps getting weirder."

"For real. But we should probably go now."

"Yeah, we should," I reply.

We walk out of the building together. When we make it to the parking lot, I stop for a minute to decompress.

"That was close," I say, "but at the same time so easy. All I had to do was this." At the moment I say "this," I snap to show Nate how easy it was.

He looks at me like I'm exploding.

"What?"

"You just fucking snapped again."

"Oh shit."

Nate and I start running down the parking lot, but before we can make it to the road, the group of villains races out of the building toward us. I try to snap again, but there's a magnetic force pulling my fingers apart. It hurts in a way I can't describe. My muscles start tensing up, and my fingers are cramping.

"Your powers reset every two hours," Daniel states, as if I should already know that. I didn't know my powers came with a limit. But I guess they're technically not my powers, since they came from the Deal and Do.

"But Nate's—"

"Let's just say there are some interesting side effects to both of your powers. It appears Nathaniel hasn't experienced those yet."

Before I can process that response, Sadie strides over with a rope and starts tying Nate and me up like she does this every day.

"Please, Sadie, you don't have to do this," I plead, trying to search for her good side. I know it's still inside her somewhere. The right person just needs to bring it back.

"Oh, honey," she says in the most condescending tone I begin to cringe, "don't you play that game with me."

Sadie continues tying us up, but I try to wrestle against it.

Out of nowhere someone whizzes through the parking lot on a motor-cycle, jumps off, frees us from the rope's trap, and ties Sadie up instead. The Deal and Do leaders begin yelling and cursing while a couple members flee in fear. It all occurs within a blink of an eye. Blond hair and freckled skin flicker past me as she fiercely battles the four remaining leaders. I stand in shock as I watch my sister, Violet, make her parents, Raymond, and Daniel run away from the scene of the night.

"Violet? Where did you—how did you—"

"There's no time to explain," she speaks sternly. "We need to get you out of here before you get yourself killed."

There's a long pause as she looks over at Nate with a questionable look on her face. Finally, she asks, "So who are you?"

"I—"

"He's Nate," I interrupt. "You guys can talk later. Like you said, we need to get out of here."

I'm still trying to wrap my mind around the surprising events of the evening as we get on Violet's motorcycle. To be honest I had no idea she even owned a motorcycle.

I'm definitely going to need a long explanation of why she's suddenly on my side.

꙳

Wind blows against my face as we round the corner. A large field comes into view. I notice four people jumping and waving at us. Only two rights and a left before we arrive at my house. But that's not where we're going. I have no idea where our destination is to be honest. Now that Sadie isn't with me anymore, I can't count on her to have the plans together.

As we get closer, I recognize the four people to be Carla, Teresa, Nala, and Trevor. Violet stops the motorcycle at the end of the field, and I run across the grass over to Trevor. We embrace in a long hug, and he kisses me briefly on the lips. I don't know why, but the kiss feels stiff and awkward, almost forced. I feel uncomfortably vulnerable hugging him in front of Nate, as if a million eyes are towering over me.

"It's so good to see you again!" I exclaim, trying to feel the same amount of butterflies I did when I last saw him, but nothing is there.

"I gotta say I was pretty worried when you sent that text."

What text? Oh wait. The last one I sent him. The one that *looked a little suspicious if you had no idea what was actually going on. goodbye I'll miss you i love you.* I have to admit that, at the moment, not even I was fully sure what was happening.

"Oh that. Yeah. I didn't really have time to send you a long text or anything."

"You look . . . different."

"Is that bad?" I question his tone.

"No, you look amazing!"

"So you're saying I didn't look amazing before?"

"No, no. I just—"

I feel a tap on my left shoulder. I turn around to see Carla beaming at me.

"Calypso!" she shrieks loudly in my ear. "Oh my god, we missed you so much! The lunch table felt so empty without you."

I barely have a chance to reply before Nala steps into view. I am so overwhelmed by all the welcoming, but at the same time, I am enjoying the attention.

"What's up, Cal?" Nala says. "How was the barn?"

I don't have enough time to figure out how she knew I was in a barn. Instead, I just reply, "Don't even get me started."

She laughs, and I ask, "Where's Teresa?"

"Oh, she's over there," Nala says and points to Teresa, who's chatting with Violet and Carla. Somehow, in the span of seconds, Carla was able to make her way back over to the other girls.

My gaze travels to Nate subconsciously. Our eyes meet, and we engage in two seconds of awkward staring. He is uncomfortably keeping his distance from everyone and fidgeting with his hands. To break the awkwardness,

I lead Trevor and Nala over to him.

"So, guys . . . this is Nate," I introduce. "He was the one that helped me stay alive all these months. Literally, if I didn't find him, I'd probably be dead. He took me to this abandoned barn he'd been staying at. It turns out he was hiding from the Deal and Do too."

Nala and Nate shake hands and exchange a few words. Trevor glares judgingly from me to Nate in silence.

"Mr. T., what's the issue?" Nala calls Trevor out. "Does this guy look like he's gonna bite?"

"Nothing, sorry," Trevor stammers. Then he turns to Nate and says, "Hey, thanks," with the fakest smile I've ever seen.

"Thank you a trillion times for taking care of our dear friend Cal," Nala adds. "I bet she was a handful."

"Totally. What's your name?"

"I'm Nala. This is Trevor. The shorter one over there is Carla, and Teresa is the pretty girl in the jean jacket, and then there's Calypso's sister, Violet. But you've already met her."

Violet, Carla, and Teresa head our way, and Nate introduces himself to them as well, then Violet looks at me. We step to the side, and I let out my thoughts.

"Why did you do this?" I question.

"Do what?"

"You know . . . save me, I guess. You know what I'm talking about. Why did you do it?"

"What do you mean?" she asks.

"Well, you know . . . we never really spoke to each other until that night before I ran away. I hardly know you. I didn't even know you had a motorcycle. I also thought you were like one of the 'cool' senior cheer girls, not someone who'd want to hang out with people like me and my friends."

"I guess a lot has changed."

"Like what? There had to be something that sparked such a drastic change."

"Well, I guess one night I heard Mom and Dad having a strange conversation downstairs . . . about you. And I knew something sketchy was going on."

"What about me?"

"Just about you and your powers and a meeting with the Deal and Do and how they were gonna stay under the radar now that more people were finding out about the company. That's why I came into your room the night before you left. I was gonna tell you, but there was a weird vibe between us. I decided that instead of bothering you, I'd go see what Mom and Dad were really doing, so I did. That's when I found out what their secret was. That's when I found out Sadie was evil."

Paths are connecting, and I'm beginning to realize the answer to my question from earlier.

"Wait, so were you the one who sent me that timeline . . . and the note in the river?"

"Oh yeah, that was me. I was trying to send you a message that Sadie was one of them. But obviously, you still didn't get that. And I knew you were following me when I went to go find Mom and Dad. I was trying to show you who they really were."

"Oh my god! You knew I was following you? I can't believe I've had it wrong this whole time."

"What do you mean?"

"Well, when I saw you enter the tent and Raymond introduced himself to you, I thought you were one of them. That's one of the biggest reasons I ran away."

"Oh my gosh, no. Raymond and Daniel . . . they all thought that one day I would be part of their team because of my parents. So when I just randomly showed up, they welcomed me like a guest. But man, were they in for a surprise. I mean, I'm surprised myself that I didn't fall for their manipulation. My parents were already manipulating me a ton, making me leave the house all the time—"

"Wait. That's why you were always gone?" I exclaim. So many surprises in one night. It's like my whole view of reality is being flipped upside down.

"Not because you were trying to avoid me?"

"Well, it wasn't like I was full-on forced. It's hard to explain. Their manipulation tactics kind of tricked me into not wanting to hang out with you. Part of it was also me just being an annoying high schooler, trying to get away from the house and spending all my time with friends. But it was mostly our parents."

Not a word comes out of my mouth. What am I supposed to say? There aren't any words to describe how I feel. Sadie wasn't really my best friend. Violet and I could have been closer if it weren't for her parents—my parents too, I guess. How do I know what to believe anymore?

"Please don't be mad at me," Violet adds. "I understand I was super mean to you, and you didn't deserve it. I know that now. But for a while I didn't. You were right. I was trying so hard to be that 'cool' senior cheer girl, but then I realized I needed to grow up and stop worrying so much about my reputation. A couple days after you ran away, I quit the cheer team, and I started talking to your friends. I'm going to the gym and working out a lot more, which has grown my self-confidence. I also took some self-defense classes now that I'm more of a vulnerable target to the Deal and Do. I know my old friends hate me now, but I don't care. I feel like I'm doing the right thing. And I want to be friends with you. I even decided to take a gap year before college so I can spend more time with you!"

I should be excited and crying and hugging her, shouldn't I? Again, I don't know how to react. It's hard to jump straight into a relationship with someone when they practically ignored you for your entire life. I know Violet had her reasons, but it feels uncomfortable to be vulnerable around her. And I just got betrayed by someone who I shared so many different emotions with. Not only that, but I still have more questions.

"So how did you get the timeline and phone and stuff in the first place?"

"Oh yeah. So right after Raymond welcomed me at the tent, I gave him a little taste of his own medicine. He was pissed. They all were. Calling me a traitor and stuff. But even that is an understatement. Anyway, I noticed the timeline in the back of the tent, so I just went for it and started running.

Raymond and Daniel were chasing me every step of the way, but that didn't stop me. That's when I saw you running through the trees. I was going to find you and tell you everything, but I couldn't catch you. I found your phone in the river though, and thankfully, it was still working. I didn't know your password though, so I had to wait until I could talk to your friends at school. Teresa thankfully remembered it, and then I was able to see the link you sent Trevor and I did some more research from there."

So that explains the yelling and running footsteps I heard. The Deal and Do wasn't even chasing me in the first place. They were chasing Violet. But it's good I made the decision to listen to my gut and run away. I still had danger living all around me, and besides, running away led me to finding Nate.

"But how did you know where I was?" I continue, spitting out questions. "And how were you able to place the message in the river, knowing I would see it?"

"I spied on most of the Deal and Do meetings, and I followed my parents to the barn the day they brought you that letter. And with the phone note, I was slightly following y'all too. I knew you would be coming back today because I heard Raymond and Daniel giving Sadie the fake plan to tell you. When you passed out, I just decided to toss the phone in the river nearby, hoping you'd find it and know it was from me. I was trying to get you to realize I was your ally, not Sadie."

I'm filled with utter shock. In the midst of all this chaos, the most random thought pops into my head. "Whatever happened to George . . . your boyfriend?"

"Oh, we broke up. I told him the news about you and the Deal and Do, and he didn't want to help. He said it was too much work, and he didn't want to waste his time. He was also just done with me in general. I guess it's fine, though. I knew we'd have to break up soon anyways because of college. And our relationship was always kind of toxic anyways."

"Oh, well, you really are the best."

We embrace in an awkward half hug. It feels strange, acting like this around someone who has been absent my whole life. After we hug, I walk back to the others so we can come up with a plan.

"First, I wanna say thank you. I literally don't know what I'd do without you guys."

They all say stuff like "No problem" or "It was nothing."

"So where are we going now?"

"We built a small clubhouse for you," Trevor boasts. "At least that's what we're calling it. It's not far from here."

That's what they were building, not some dumb ditch Sadie claimed they were making. But also, a clubhouse? I would never be able to do that.

"Wow, are you serious? How did y'all do it?"

"We all helped cut the wood," Carla explains. "Trevor put it together, Teresa painted it, and Violet got all the decorations."

"It was that easy?"

"My parents also helped with a lot of it. My dad came over several times especially during the building process. And we did different fundraisers to get more money for supplies."

I'm filled with the most inexpressible feelings. No way my friends went through all that shit just for me. I look back at Nate with shock, but he just gives me a "Why you looking at me?" face.

"Okay, but this is crazy," I say. "You guys did not need to do all that."

"We wanted to," Violet says.

"Well, this has been nice, but are you tired, or what?" Nala interrupts the conversation. "I know I am, and I didn't have to sleep in a barn for two months."

I laugh wearily, growing aware of the heavy exhaustion bearing down on my shoulders. "Yeah, that's true."

"Well then, what are we waiting for? Let's get out of here!"

All I can think of as I walk with Nate and Violet back to her motorcycle is how empty I feel without Sadie but also how loved and supported I feel by the rest of my friends. All these emotions are driving me crazy, but at least I'm not alone.

CHAPTER 25
SELF-AFFIRMATION

Nate and I ride out with Violet on her motorcycle, while Trevor, Carla, Teresa, and Nala get on their bikes. The relief I feel from not using my feet as transportation is unexplainable. I've been so used to walking and running all the time, but now I can finally sit and breathe as Violet drives. It's an alleviating shift back to normalcy. after about five minutes, we stop by the edge of the woods. We have to wait a few minutes for everyone else to catch up. This gives me some time to talk to Nate alone as Violet leans against the motorcycle scrolling on her phone.

"So that whole introduction thing just wasn't awkward," Nate begins.

"Yeah, sorry. I wasn't really expecting all this to go the way it did."

"For real. Can we talk about your sister saving us or whatever? Like that's one hell of a story right there."

"Yeah, I was shocked too. But I guess, one night she had heard—"

"I already know, remember? I can read her mind. I was just saying how crazy that all is."

"Oh yeah, I know."

It's weird that Nate can read my friends' minds. He probably knows more about all of them combined than I do, even though he just met them tonight.

"About Sadie . . ." Nate continues. "I'm sorry."

"Why are you sorry?"

"Not like that, just—I know y'all were close. Or at least you thought so.

I can't imagine how hurt you must be feeling right now."

"Yeah . . . I'm also just pissed at myself for not seeing this before. You were suspicious of her at first, but I couldn't get over myself. I swore so many times that she would do anything for me. It's pathetic."

"It's not pathetic, okay? And don't go off of my first reaction. I'm always like that about new people, especially after being alone for so long. But I really thought she was gonna save us too."

"Yeah."

I gaze at the grass and dirt under me as I clamp my teeth down on my cheek. Sadie was reserved, but also innocent and thoughtful and . . . she would never do something like this. All of a sudden, she's this loud, vicious sidekick for two psychopaths. What happened to her? Or was I just clueless this whole time?

"Trevor seemed real thrilled to see me," Nate mutters in the nighttime silence of crickets and bugs.

Yet another complicated person. Trevor. The only thing is, he didn't betray me like Sadie. But he's still complicated. "I know, I know. I don't understand why he's being so awkward. I'll talk to him about it later."

"Personally, I think he's a bit of an asshole."

"Excuse me? I never asked—"

I am interrupted by the rest of the group appearing on their bikes. The girls rush over to us, but Trevor stares skeptically at Nate. Not this again. I motion for him to stop the staring and actually walk over to us. He aggressively shoves himself between Nate and me.

"What did you do that for?" I whisper.

"Do what?" I throw him a look, and he quickly replies, "I don't know. I think there's something up with this guy . . . I mean, he looks suspicious. Maybe you should stop hanging out with him."

"Are you serious right now? First of all, you don't tell me what I can and can't do. Second of all, there's nothing wrong with Nate. He's just quiet. So why don't you stop being so weird?"

Trevor doesn't reply. I know he's jealous of Nate, but that's not my problem. Part of me is beginning to agree with Nate's opinion of him, but part of me doesn't want to.

Hopefully, it's just a phase. Trevor has a hard time processing his emotions because of his relationships at home. I just need to give him some time.

After wandering through the woods for another minute or two, we end up in a field surrounded by large trees. In the center of the field is a narrow wooden cabin. I run up to it and step onto the small porch. I notice two red plush benches on my right, which are the same color as the door in front of me.

"I got those benches from my aunt's house," Teresa says.

"This is really cool, you guys."

"I knew you'd like it!" Carla cheers from behind me.

"Why wouldn't she?" Trevor asks.

"Let's go inside," Violet says. "I want Cal to see what we did."

Nala opens the door and flips on a switch to her left. Bright blue lights blind my eyes.

"Sorry for the terrible lighting," Teresa apologizes. "The other lights were so expensive."

"That's okay. I don't care. I'm just grateful y'all did this."

"It's pretty in the daytime, though," Violet adds.

We walk down the hallway a couple of steps before we reach a door.

Trevor opens it and declares, "This is the sleeping room. There's a closet here for your clothing and then there's all this space for us to sleep. We brought enough air mattresses for each of us to have our own bed."

From the looks of it, the air mattresses will be crammed, but we should all be able to fit in here. The wooden walls are painted with teal, yellow, and red flowers. Teresa is quite the artist.

"I can't wait to be sleeping somewhere other than an old horse stable for once."

"Same. Especially after being there for three years," Nate says.

"Oh my god! You were there for three years?" Nala exclaims.

"I sure was."

"I can't imagine," Violet says.

"How did you even stay sane that whole time?" Teresa asks.

"It's in times of solitude where you find your wisdom," Carla says with a bizarre smile on her face.

"Okay, now let's check out the kitchen," Trevor interrupts.

"Wait," Teresa says. "What about the bathroom?"

"Well, it's not really . . ."

"What?" I ask, confused why Trevor is acting so weird.

"Trevor and Mr. Robinson were trying to work on making a real bathroom," Teresa says as she guides me through the sleeping room and to another wooden door. "But getting all the pipes installed for the toilet and sink were quite advanced. So we just have this shitty mirror and a table if you ever wanna come in here and . . . look at yourself."

I laugh at her comedic tone. But I understand what she's implying. Although I could brush my hair in here, outside in the trees is where my imaginary toilet is actually located. There's nothing wrong with that. I had to do the same thing at the barn.

"But I've been watching some more videos lately," Trevor says. "Hopefully soon this can become a real bathroom."

We return back to the hall and enter an open space. To the left is a brown table with six wooden chairs, all different styles, facing it. I recognize three of the chairs from Carla's house. To the right is a table with pictures of my friends and me on it. Across from the picture table are two yellow beanbags.

The wall to the right of the beanbags is mainly clear glass. It's not the nicest looking window, but the good thing is, there will be natural light shining through in the daytime.

"I still can't believe you guys did this. It means so much to me . . . and Nate too."

The face Trevor makes when I say Nate's name shows how much he doesn't want him to be here.

Everyone is asleep except me. I tiptoe around the scattered air mattresses and out to the porch. As I gaze up at the stars, I begin to think about the future. What am I even doing with my life at this point? I have no family. I'm living in a small shack with my friends. College and a serious career aren't even an option for me anymore. I wish I could skip ahead and see where I'm going to be in five years. I'll be nineteen years old. Five years feels so far away but so close at the same time. Will the Deal and Do still be chasing me? Will I be living in this clubhouse with my friends? What if I don't live long enough to be nineteen? What if the Deal and Do catches me before then?

I hear the door creak open behind me. I glance back to see Teresa walking out in gray sweatpants and a pastel purple crew neck. She sits beside me.

"It's been weird not having you in my life for the past two months," she says.

"I know. You really need to catch me up."

"And you need to catch me up. What all happened while you were away?"

"That's true." I laugh before adding, "Well, I figured out what my powers were."

"I know," she says, surprising me.

"What? How?"

"Violet told us."

"Oh right, yeah."

"And obviously, that explains why we felt so weird at Carla's house. You know, that day before you left."

"Oh yeah. That feels like forever ago. I'm sorry I didn't tell you guys about my powers. I was just so shocked, and I didn't know what to say or who to trust."

"It's okay. You don't need to be sorry. You had every right to be scared."

I nod as I begin to think through all the terrifying situations I have faced. Barely enough time has occurred for me to process the events of the past few months. Now that Teresa reminded me of that day, some buried feelings are resurfacing. I don't want to reflect on those ugly, complex emotions at the moment, so I take a deep breath, regaining control over my thoughts.

"So tell me. What have I missed?"

"Well . . . um . . . where do I even start? I guess Spencer has been causing more drama at school. The other day he was walking through the halls with his new friends blaring music and he 'accidentally' tripped me."

Her tone on "accidentally" makes it clear he did it on purpose.

"Usual Spencer."

"For real, and he keeps calling me a fat, ugly bitch and stuff. In math, him and his one friend—I forgot his name—always come up to me and make fun of how I doodle on my paper. They're like, 'Oh you think you're so quirky,' or whatever. It just pisses me off. Spencer acts like he didn't used to sit with us at lunch a few months ago."

"Oh my god, that's so annoying. Why is he being so rude to you? You're not even trying to engage with him, right?"

"No, I'm always avoiding him as much as possible."

"Exactly, so the fact that he's literally coming out of his way to say shit to you like that is so stupid."

"I know. I just try my best to not let it get to me."

"That sucks though. If I had been here, I would've done something. He has no right."

"Yeah, Nala hates him with a burning passion because of everything he says about me, so she tries to tell him off, but he never listens. I really don't get it. I was barely even a part of the whole Sadie drama, but I guess he just loves to make fun of people like me."

"What do you mean people like you? None of this is your fault."

"I know. Anyways, to change the subject, I got my license in October."

"Oh yeah, that's right! Now you can drive me places."

"Well, not yet. Not until April. Gotta wait six months, you know."

"True, but still . . . What else?"

"Well, Nala and I are kind of official now." She continues, a large grin spreading across her face. "We went to homecoming together."

"You did? What did your parents say?"

"They didn't know. I just told them I was going with a couple of friends.

And to make them believe me more, Nala, Violet, and Carla came to pick me up, and Violet drove us there."

"It feels weird having Violet in our friend group now."

"Yeah, I don't know. She definitely wasn't the nicest person before you left, but I can tell she's trying to get better. And I think she's doing a good job. She's so nice and funny and she's helped me through a lot of personal things while you've been gone."

I get Teresa's point, but I'm still a little irritated. Violet replaced me. If I'd been here, I could've grown closer to Teresa, but now she likes Violet more than me. I need to fix that.

"So your parents still don't know about you and Nala?"

A nervous frown appears on her face.

"Oh no. What happened?"

"Well, starting around the end of October, I was letting Nala come over to my house to hang out and stuff when I was home alone. One day my parents came home when Nala was leaving and asked who she was, but I just told them she was a friend from school, and we were studying together for chem. Everything was fine until about two weeks ago when I was in my room minding my own business, and my stupid mother came in and yelled at me." She takes a small pause before continuing. "She found footage on the security camera of me and Nala kissing on the couch. And see, if it were a boy, she'd be fine, but because it was a girl, my mom took my phone for two weeks, and she wrote down a long list of all these rules I need to follow. She's trying to make me straight again or something, but it's like, I can't change my feelings."

"God, that is so stupid. You didn't even do anything bad."

"I know. And my stepdad gave me a long lecture about what it means to be a true woman, which is so fucking messed up because he isn't even a girl himself. What does he know?"

"What the hell. A true woman? Your parents are actually so annoying."

"For real. I was telling Nala the other day how much my mom resents me. It's not even because of anything I've done. I'm just a reminder of her past relationship and she holds that grudge against me for some reason. Then my stepdad, which you already kind of know, is literally the epitome of a traditional Southern man. Like he's so homophobic and racist and he's always making stupid, 'Kids these days . . .' comments."

"God, those guys are so annoying. Like sorry, but we can't live the same way your grandparents did. Things have changed."

"Exactly. It also pisses me off how nice they are to my brothers. I get that those are actually my stepdad's kids, but I'm still part of the family. It's just not fair."

"I know it's not. My parents used to favor Violet too, but I mean, that whole situation is different."

"Yeah. I was just so angry and upset after that day when they yelled at me. I came to school the next day in tears."

"Oh my god. I'm so sorry I wasn't here to help, but I'm here to support you now," I say and embrace her in a long and thoughtful hug.

"I don't deserve a friend like you," she sniffles.

"You spend so much time affirming others," I whisper in her ear. "It's time you start affirming yourself."

CHAPTER 26
MY WORST NIGHTMARE

I jolt awake, panting loudly. I try to tell myself it was just another night-mare as I slow down my breathing. after my conversation with Teresa, I only gained about three hours of sleep, and now I'm awake again. I sigh, still trying to wrap my head around Sadie's turn to darkness. All this new shocking information being slapped in my face the moment I return is so overwhelming.

I glance at Violet's back as she rolls over on the air mattress next to me. Her phone is in between us. I turn it over and look at the time—5:13 a.m. I decide there's no use in me going back to bed if I'm only going to sit there wrestling with my anxious thoughts. I quietly step into the hallway. I sit down on one of the beanbag chairs, the one closest to the kitchen. I ponder over my conversation with Sadie last night. I wish I had said more, but I felt so hurt. I've always been there for her. What made her want to betray me? What did I ever do to her? According to the timeline, she joined the Deal and Do on July 17. I saw her twice between that day and the start of the school year. It was the beginning of her strange, new attitude. She avoided interacting with me during our sleepover, and when we went to The Outlets on July 22, she claimed she felt sick and that we needed to leave early.

I wish I had figured out her secret sooner. I was beginning to, but she played it off with her sob story, and I couldn't see past the fact that every-thing was normal again. I'm so angry at myself. If only I could turn back time and change my actions.

At the same time, I am so bewildered. I remember going over to Sadie's house to apologize the day Spencer hit me. She sounded so genuine with her response when she told me she was sorry. And then she invited me into her house to hang out afterward. I thought we were back on good terms, especially after our last sleepover when we stayed up until 2:00 a.m. She looked like she was having fun, laughing and talking. No way that was all an act. But I don't know, maybe it was. Now I don't know if I'll ever be able to trust anyone the same way again.

I peer down at my blue sweater, the same sweater I've been wearing for a month. It's covered in mud, dirt, and other filth. I used to care so much about my appearance, but I haven't seen a mirror in months. Not until today, but even then, I wasn't focusing on how I looked. I've gazed at my reflection in ponds and creeks; there's been no time for me to care about my looks. Maybe that's a good thing. It's your inner beauty that truly matters. People used to tell me that all the time, especially when I was in middle school. I never took them seriously. Who wants to look ugly in front of their friends? No one. But the truest friends don't give a shit about how you look on the outside, and if they do, they're not meant to be your friend.

There's something that suddenly sparks an interest in my mind. I was so full of adrenaline during the chaos at the school that I didn't have time to think about the side conversations everyone was having, but now, as I'm reviewing the details, I recall three words coming out of Sadie's mouth right before I froze time. *I told you.* Sadie said that after Raymond and Daniel realized Nate was still alive. She knew. And she told them. They must not have believed her at the time. How interesting. She acts like she has all this power now, but do the Deal and Do leaders even take her seriously?

I think again about that day at the barn. When Sadie showed up. There was something else strange about that day. I can't quite remember. The days at the barn blur together in my mind now. Every day had a similar routine. Wake up, sit outside and watch the sunrise, eat random shit for breakfast, talk to Nate, run, sit around, more random shit for dinner, talk to Nate more, sleep. Repeat. I think through all those activities in my head. Then it hits me. When Nate and I were on a run earlier that day, I saw people watching us. Three silhouettes in the distance—Raymond, Daniel, and Sadie. Or Sally, as they call her. Sadie told me Nala's brother drove her to the barn, which would make no sense. Sadie and Nala barely talked to each other.

I hear the sleeping room door open, and Violet steps into view a moment later.

"Oh hey," she says. "I didn't know you were up already."

"Couldn't sleep."

"The whole Sadie situation must be bugging you."

"Yeah."

"Do you wanna talk about it?"

No, I don't want to talk about it at all, especially with Violet. She's been absent my entire life, and now she's expecting me to have deep, personal conversations with her. Relationships like this can't be forced.

But I don't say any of that. I just stare at the floor, thinking about how much I need new shoes.

"It'll be okay." Violet continues, although I never said I wanted a conversation. In fact, I didn't answer her at all. Shouldn't she get the gist? "You'll get through this. You're strong."

At that, I scoff. "You don't even know me."

She looks a little hurt by my words. What was she expecting? For me to forget her past behavior? Last time I saw her, we knew nothing about each other. This all is taking a lot to get used to, and I don't think I'm ready for her to be a part of my life yet.

"Well, why don't you try to get some sleep?" Violet smiles lightly. "You need to stay energized."

I nod and curl up in the beanbag. She heads into the kitchen and gets a snack. I keep waiting for her to leave, but she doesn't. She just stands there munching on a protein bar. So I sit in the beanbag, pretending to be asleep. There's nothing better to do with my life anyways.

CHAPTER 27
WHAT IT TAKES TO SURVIVE

"They're usually gone around this time. I'm not sure what's taking so long," Violet says.

The two of us are hiding behind a bush near our old house. It's weird remembering how I used to live there and feel at ease. This was the place I returned to at the end of every day. I might still be living there if it weren't for the school newspaper revealing my power or the single decision I made to run away. But no longer is this my home. No longer is this my safe haven.

We are spying on Violet's parents, Stephanie and Dave. From now on, I've decided to call them by their actual names. I feel awkward calling them my parents. I don't think of them as authority figures anymore and they don't deserve my respect. They never even wanted me as their child anyways. They never cared about me. It was just part of their job to keep me in their sight. Literally. Raymond and Daniel handed me over to them so I could still be in the eyes of the company. I was only a small child. I had no idea what kind of evil was out there.

I wasn't looking forward to coming back here, scared of interacting with Stephanie and Dave. When Violet first brought up the idea, I completely refused. But I finally decided it was better to get some of my old clothes and belongings rather than waste the little money we have on new ones.

"We've been sitting here for almost thirty minutes. Why don't we just go back?" I ask. "We can try this again tomorrow."

"No, no. We're already here. Let's just wait a few more minutes."

"And a few minutes turns into an hour, then a few more hours after that, and soon, we're sitting here for the whole d—"

"Would you please stop? Just try and have a little bit of optimism."

"I wish." I laugh in a dry, sarcastic tone.

"Stop being so difficult. I'm telling you, they're my parents. And I was already spying on them when you were gone. I think I have their schedule pretty much memorized."

"Yeah, I know. You've mentioned this like three times now."

Violet rolls her eyes. "They were supposed to be at the headquarters for a daily meeting at one o'clock. They must be running la—Oh wait, here they are. Look, look."

I shift my attention over to the driveway. Stephanie is bickering loudly at Dave.

"You know what Ray is gonna say when he hears you slept in this morning? You need to take these meetings more seriously!"

"Quit your yapping! I take these meetings very seriously. You just don't understand how special male-to-male relationships can be, Steph. He'll have sympathy for me."

"I never realized how horrible he treated women," I whisper to Violet. It's not just the words he's saying that make his presence so demeaning, it's the condescending tone and attitude he's wearing.

"Yeah, me neither. Not until after you left. I saw him make a few comments to Mom before, but they were very subtle. I definitely think he was trying to stay under the radar around us."

Stephanie begins to walk over to the driver's side, but Dave pushes her and growls, "I know how to drive, for God's sake."

Dave slams the car, backs out of the driveway, and speeds down the street.

Violet holds up her pointer finger, signaling for me to wait.

"Okay, all clear," she says, and we creep around to the back door.

Thank God Stephanie and Dave haven't installed cameras. Not yet, at least.

We enter the house, and a weird aroma I can't describe enters my nostrils. All I know is it smells like home. Everything looks about the same as it did before, except for the fake white Christmas tree in the living room and more scattered piles of paperwork than I remember. Now that I'm gone, Stephanie and Dave don't have to hide all their junk in the office.

Violet immediately heads up the stairs. I'm about to follow, but when I notice the seventy dollars of cash on the island, I can't help myself. It's not like a seventy dollar loss will affect Stephanie and Dave. They're already super rich from working with the Deal and Do. I'm the one who actually needs money to survive. I hide the cash in my jacket pocket and run up the stairs. Violet is in her room, gathering a couple of clothing items and a blanket. This isn't her first time back to grab old things of hers, so she doesn't need as much as me.

I enter my room. It feels strange being here. The vision in my head of my bedroom became so distorted over time, I feel like this isn't the same room I left behind. But nothing has changed, except for me. I rush over to the closet and find an old duffel bag. I set it on my bed and toss five shirts, three pants, two shorts, socks, a bra, and panties in it, as well as a gray hoodie. Then I head into my bathroom and get my makeup, deodorant, toothbrush, and hairbrush. I also add my Bob Ross pencil, a pencil sharpener, my art journal, and the old stuffed bear, Freddy, which I've had since I was seven, before closing up my bag.

I walk back into the hallway and meet Violet at the top of the stairs. We silently exit the house together. Technically, we just performed a breaking and entering. But I don't care. At the end of the day, I will do anything it takes to survive.

CHAPTER 28
YOU HAVE TO CHOOSE

Today is January 5, 2015. I'm getting ready to go to school for the first time in four months. We thought I should wait until after Christmas break instead of randomly jumping back in. It'll definitely feel weird returning to the normal routine. It's going to be even weirder walking in the school halls with Nate. Through the help of Carla's parents and Violet, he is now enrolled at Brevard High School in tenth grade.

Christmas this year was different than usual. In the past it was the one day the Greshams and I acted like a normal, happy family. It felt fake and awkward. It might seem that Christmas would've been worse this year because there weren't as many gifts and we weren't in a nice, warm home, but being with my friends made the holiday so much better.

Nate and I weren't able to get gifts for anyone, but Carla, Teresa, Nala, and Trevor each bought one gift for all of us. Carla gave me a new backpack, Teresa bought me a coloring book, Nala gave me a fancy box of crayons to go with Teresa's gift, and Trevor got me a pair of Bob Ross socks. after opening the gifts, we drank hot cocoa that Nala had brought from their house and relaxed on the porch. Violet didn't contribute much to the giftgiving. Except later, when no one else was around, she gave Nate and me a small share of money to save for essentials.

While we were sitting around with our hot cocoa, Nala came out as non-binary. They were already talking about it with Teresa weeks before that, trying to sort out their feelings. We were all really supportive and encouraging as Nala made the announcement, so I think that lifted their spirits. A few days later, Nala returned to the clubhouse with their long dreads cut into a short poof of hair on the top of their head.

The new haircut is definitely helping them ease into their true identity.

After my first week back, Carla, Nala, and Teresa started sleeping at their own houses and returned to the clubhouse during the day. Trevor has yet to do the same. I'm pretty sure he stays so he doesn't leave Nate and me out of his sight. It's very strange. He has a house to sleep in, and Nate doesn't. It's not like anything bad will happen if he leaves. Now that Teresa, Nala, and Carla leave at night, Violet and I use the sleeping room, and Trevor and Nate sleep on the beanbag chairs.

"Hurry up, Cal!" Teresa shouts from outside the bedroom door.

I take one last glance at my reflection before I grab my backpack, which is such a dark shade of navy it looks black from afar. I speed out the door, into the hallway, and outside with the rest of the crew. The sun is just barely peeking through the depths of the lush evergreen trees.

"You look more awake than usual," Nala says.

I laugh at that. I don't think I look awake at all but whatever.

"I can't believe you're finally going to be back at school again," Trevor says with a grin.

"We better get going," Carla says. "We don't want to be late for y'all's first day back!"

Entering the school's main entrance, into the cafeteria and through the hallway sends me flashbacks from last month when I thought Sadie was saving us. How stupid I was to put my trust in her. I wish I knew why she betrayed me. What did I ever do? I guess I did humiliate her in front of the entire cafeteria, but that was after she was already with the Deal and Do. What urged her to turn to the other side?

I put my hands in the pockets of my jacket and walk quickly down the hall. I say goodbye to Violet, Teresa, Nate, and Nala. Pushing through the crowd of people distracts me, and suddenly, I bump into someone.

"Oh my gosh. I'm so sorry!" I apologize clumsily while picking my math book off the ground.

Then I hear that chilling voice. The one that's been haunting my nightmares for a whole month now. The voice of a stranger that I once knew.

"Don't be," she speaks.

My heart sinks as I quickly stand back up and avoid Sadie's sharp green eyes. "Oh, it's you."

I glare at her from head to toe. I have to crane my head up to look at her face. We used to make jokes about our height difference, but now it's actually intimidating. Anger boils up inside me. Sadie betrayed me in a way I can't describe. The pain I feel is so complex.

"Cal . . . can we please talk? Alone?"

"Why would I want to talk to the person who was my best friend, then constantly lied to me and said she was saving me when she only did the opposite? You betrayed me!"

My face grows hot, and a waterfall of tears streams out of my eyes. I'm not trying to be dramatic or cry, but I can't help myself. I can feel the enmity rumbling through my chest, boiling up like lava. Soon, the volcano is going to explode. How will I be able to control it? I'm not the bad guy. I'm just angry. But what if my anger turns me into a monster? No, I won't let that happen. Everyone in the hall is staring at us now. Embarrassment floods over me. It's my first day back, and I only feel like we're repeating the day Spencer hit me.

"Cal, I really am truly sorry and—"

"Why should I believe you?" I growl over my tears.

"I—"

"I don't think a single person in this building has any reason to trust you after what you did to me!"

"Cal, please listen—"

I shove myself through the crowd and shout at Sadie, "I'm never listening to you again!"

Sadie continues to follow me. Why can't she just leave me alone? She yanks my arm and pulls me into the empty art classroom.

"Get your stupid hand off me," I snarl when we are out of everyone's sight. Sadie quickly places her hand off my arm and by her side. A long, heavy silence fills the room, the scratchy buzz of the AC humming through my ears. I need to blow my nose, but I see no tissue around, so I just suck in the snots. I decide now is a good time to ask Sadie about her intentions.

"Why did you do it? What was in it for you? Everyone hates you now, just so you know."

"Thanks for the update."

"Why did you do it? Answer my question."

"I had to. It was the only thing that could keep me alive."

"Oh really?"

"I mean, you would love them," she adds, completely veering away from our original conversation. "Daniel and Raymond aren't as bad as they seem. I have my own mansion now with servants and everything. I'm living true luxury. It's so perfect!"

"I'm not falling for your traps anymore. And sorry to break it to you, but you can't be friends with the hero and the villain at the same time. You have to choose, and it looks like you already have."

I bolt out the door and head to the bathroom before my first class. Looking in the mirror, I can see that my eyes are red and puffy. I look terrible. I cup my hands together and pour cold sink water into them. I splash the frigid water on my face and take a long, relieving breath. Then I grab a few paper towels to wipe my face and blow my nose. I check my reflection again. I don't look great, but I'm still here. I may be fragile, but I am not broken. Not yet, at least. I rush out of the bathroom and hurry to my class. I run swiftly since I'm already fifteen minutes late.

CHAPTER 29
THE BOY I LOVED

Trevor and I meet up with the rest of our friends on our way to the cafeteria.

"How has your first day back been?" Violet asks.

"It was okay," I answer, avoiding her eyes.

Part of me wants to tell her about my interaction with Sadie, but things are still weird between us. One second she barely talks to me; the next thing you know, I see her 24/7.

"That's not very convincing. What happened?"

"Does this have to do with you being late to class this morning?" Carla inquires.

"You were late?" Violet exclaims like it's the end of the world. "But how? What happened?"

"Let's get to the cafeteria first. We can talk about it there."

When we make it inside, I grab a tray with a slice of soggy school pizza and head over to our usual table.

"So," Trevor begins, "what's going on?"

I sigh heavily. "I bumped into Sadie on the way to my locker. She started arguing with me in front of everyone. I can't believe you guys didn't see it."

"Sorry," Carla apologizes guiltily. "I went to class early and figured you'd be there soon."

"It's okay."

"What was she saying?" Nate wonders.

"Things like 'I'm sorry' and 'I really didn't want to hurt your feelings.' She was trying to make me pity her or whatever. I kept telling her I didn't wanna listen. I even tried walking away, but she would not leave me alone. We ended up in the art room, and that's when I asked her why she betrayed me. She said it was the only thing to keep her alive."

"'Keep her alive'? What does that mean?" Carla asks.

"Maybe they threatened her or something, I don't know," Teresa adds.

"That's what I was wondering. But when I asked her more, she didn't even answer. She just went through this whole thing of how I would love Raymond and Daniel. They apparently gave her some sort of fancy mansion."

"Of course they did," Nala comments.

"What else did she say?" Nate asks.

"She wanted me to come with her. I'm pretty sure that was Raymond and Daniel's idea. They wanted her to bribe me again so I would go with her to the Deal and Do. But I didn't fall for any of it. It's all bullshit."

"I'm so sorry. I wish we could've been there to help," Teresa says.

"I think if Sadie just took a couple chill pills and a nice sauna, she'd be good," Nala jokes. Nala is always joking. There's never a time when you can have a real, deep conversation with them. Maybe that's not the case when they're only with Teresa, but sometimes I wish they could be more understanding. Not everything has to be funny for life to be enjoyable.

"Ever since you told me about her, I knew she was a lying bitch," Nate mutters.

"I know. It's all my fault. All this time you could sense she was bad, and I never wanted to listen to you."

"It's not your fault at all. I was never blaming you; it just pisses me off the way she treats you."

"It still makes me sad," Carla says with a frown. "Sadie was such a good friend . . . and those men tore every inch of her apart."

I cover my face with my hands to stop the oncoming tears.

"Oh, Cal," Carla says, wrapping her arm around me. "Don't take it personal. You did nothing wrong."

"Of course, you didn't," Trevor says. "Why would you?"

We're sitting in Carla's living room, the TV murmuring in the background. Carla and Violet are on the two armchairs across from each other. Teresa and Nala are cuddled under a blanket on one side of the couch. I'm squeezed in between Nate and Trevor on the other side—as if there couldn't be a more awkward place to sit. Teresa and Nate are complaining about their math teacher when the TV automatically switches to the news.

The stern newscaster reports, "After damaging items and harassing shoppers in four stores at The Outlets of Transylvania County in downtown Brevard, Raymond Macon and Daniel Smith, along with their teenage assistant, Sally Lovington, are nowhere to be found. Seven employees were injured in the attack. Multiple windows were shattered and store items broken. Local police have traced down all their last known locations. Raymond, Daniel, and Sally are known to be quite dangerous. Lieutenant Kramer at the Transylvania County Police Department has interrogated other members of the Deal and Do Company, but no one knows the location of their leaders. Wherever they are, they're suspected to have weapons. Please be on the lookout for these criminals. They could be anywhere by now—" Teresa shuts off the TV.

"Oh my gosh, that's horrible! Seven innocent employees injured!" Violet exclaims. "Why would they do that?"

"I don't know. Why would they do any of the shit they've done?" I say. "Raymond and Daniel are literal psychopaths—thinking they can take over the world and stuff."

"Okay, but why does it matter now?" Trevor questions. "They're gone. They're obviously not in Brevard because no one's found them. For now, we don't need to worry."

Nate scoffs. "What the hell kinda logic is that? We always need to worry.

Just because no one has found them doesn't mean they've completely vanished. And who knows when we'll see them again. In ten minutes they could walk right through that door and you would be dead because you're living in a fantasy."

"'Living in a fantasy'? You're hilarious, trying to make this into some dramatic movie scene. I keep telling you Cal, this guy is so paranoid 24/7. I'm just trying to maintain some positivity and stay calm, but of course Nate has to come in with, 'We're all gonna die. The world is ending.' Just shut the fuck up."

Trevor is being unreasonably immature right now, but the truth is, I used to have the same attitude. I never wanted to face the darkness in life. I wanted to live the "teenage dream" and forget that the world is corrupt; forget that I'm running, fighting for my life. But doing that gets yourself killed. Just like Nate told me months ago. I've finally accepted what my life is now. Trevor needs to take off his imaginary blindfold and do the same.

"What the hell?" Teresa exclaims. "You are being so stubborn right now."

Trevor stands. "I am not stubborn! I'm trying to still live a good life!"

"This isn't about you right now," Nate continues and steps up from the couch to face Trevor. "This is about Cal and keeping her safe. It's about keeping all of us safe in general. We don't know where Raymond, Daniel, and Sadie are right now. Knowing them, they could come back any minute and fight us with more strength, more weapons, and more violence. They want to weaken us. Especially me and Cal. If Calypso is your girlfriend, don't you want her to stay safe?"

"Just stop. I know you're trying to make me look bad."

"I'm not trying to do anything. You're the one making yourself look like a big baby right now."

Trevor walks up to Nate. "I swear, you just can't stop yourself."

"Woah, woah, woah!" Nala tries to go in between them, but Teresa puts her hand in front of Nala, keeping them back. "Trev, c'mon. You're taking this too far. You don't need to make a scene."

"Yeah, back off," Nate says as he pushes Trevor away from him.

"I'm not making a scene!" Trevor yells and pushes Nate more aggressively.

"What the fuck dude?" Nate laughs. "This is so dumb. I can't believe you're doing this right now."

I run in between them before Trevor makes another move.

"Guys! Sit down. This is crazy! We're supposed to be friends. We're supposed to support each other and stuff. It doesn't need to be like this."

"Yeah, whatever," Trevor mutters, embarrassed but trying to hide it. "It's over now."

Nate holds back his shocked laughter. We sit back down, tension still in the air. Violet asks a question, attempting to start a new conversation, but I can't even focus.

"I'm gonna go to the bathroom real quick," I say under my breath as I stand up and walk quickly down the hall.

We finally finished our homework together and now the only people left at the house are Trevor, Carla, Teresa, and me. I'm still shaken up by Trevor's reaction earlier. That was so unlike him. But I'm beginning to wonder if that was actually the real version of him. What if this whole time since we started dating, he's been covering up his true colors with a mask?

Mrs. Robinson steps into the room and asks, "How's everyone doing? Would any of y'all like some water?"

"Yes, please!" Carla says.

"Yeah, I'll have some too," Teresa adds. "Thank you."

Mrs. Robinson looks at me. "No, I'm good. Thanks."

"You are so brave, you know. Carla is always telling me about you, all the stuff you've been through and how well you adapt to change."

"Oh, really? That's so sweet," I beam with genuine joy. I didn't know any of my friends talked about me that much.

"I'm just glad Carla has a friend like you."

I don't know what I ever did to earn Mrs. Robinson's overwhelming kindness. I watch as she sits on the couch with the other two girls and sparks conversation.

Trevor returns from the bathroom and appears behind me.

I turn to him and mutter, "What was your deal earlier? There was no reason for that to turn into an argument. Nate—"

"So you're on his side now?"

"No, it's not like that. What has gotten into you since I left? From the moment I came back, you've been so immature, giving Nate mean glares, pushing him the way you did. You aren't the Trevor I used to know."

"I'm telling you, I don't like the looks of that guy. He's—"

"I don't remember asking for your opinion."

"I know, but I'm just saying he—like did you see—I swear—"

"I just think you're jealous."

"I'm not. I—"

"Whatever is going on with you, it needs to stop, and you need to fix yourself. 'Cause if you still want us, you need to start acting more like the boy I loved."

With that said, I walk out the door and all the way back to the clubhouse, the anger and sadness revealing itself.

CHAPTER 30
LOCKED BRAIN

I step inside, the low muffle of Violet and Nate's voices traveling through the hallway. I walk toward the kitchen and set my backpack by the counter. Nate and Violet are relaxing on the beanbag chairs.

"Hey, Cal. Is everything okay?" Nate asks.

"Yeah, I'm fine. I just need some time alone."

"Where's Trevor?" Violet asks.

"I really don't wanna talk about this right now."

Nate and Violet exchange looks, and I walk away. When I enter the sleeping room, I sulk over to the wooden wall and slouch against it. An overwhelming frustration overtakes me. Nate was only backing me up, and Trevor got so uptight for no reason.

That's not at all how I remembered him. To me, he was witty, caring, and understanding. Something has gotten into him, and now he's grown more immature, careless, and hurtful. I don't even want to talk to him because it's as if I'm speaking to a stranger.

There is a knock on the door.

"Who is it?" I ask.

"It's me." Nate's deep, calming voice seeps through.

"Come in."

He trudges over and sits next to me.

"Are you okay?" he asks.

"I guess. What about you?"

"I'm fine. It's not like I just got attacked."

"I know, I'm sorry. I didn't know—"

"Don't worry about me. Seriously, I am fine, but I'm telling you, you two need to separate. He's pretty toxic, if you ask me."

My stomach recoils at Nate's words. Deep inside, I can sense he's right, but he doesn't know Trevor like I do. I don't think he will be like this forever. It also makes me uncomfortable hearing Nate tell me what I should do about this. Yes, I know Nate can read his mind and that he doesn't like Trevor, but I can't ignore the feeling it might be more than that. Maybe Nate is trying to separate Trevor and me for his own good. I don't want that. No one gets to dictate my choices.

Nate, noticing my silence, changes the subject. "Anyway, since we are both on the same page about the Deal and Do, I think we should make a plan."

"Yeah, that's a good idea. I was already kinda thinking about it."

"Okay, so what do you have in mind?"

"Well, if they show up here, that's easy. All we need to do is sneak out the back, run through the trees, and leave. If they show up at school, we can't run. We'll have to fight back."

"Okay, how?" Nate asks.

"I don't know. It depends where we are in the school."

"I doubt they'll barge into a classroom or anything like that since everyone is already looking for them."

"Yeah, true," I reply. "So . . . let's say they find us in the hallway, at a time when it's less crowded."

"That seems accurate."

"We let them fight us first to make it look like they're winning. Then we free ourselves and . . ."

"And what?"

"We'd need a weapon."

"Um . . . good point. What about . . . wait a sec, what about chairs?"

"Chairs?" I question. "You wanna fight them with chairs? Are you serious right now?"

"I mean, if we're at school, that would be our best bet. Chairs are everywhere."

"Okay, I guess you're right. That may work. So we'd get the chairs and throw them at Raymond and Daniel and whoever else is there. Then, when they're knocked out, we call the cops and get these shitheads arrested."

"Yeah. We're coming for you, bastards."

I laugh and a slight pause occurs in the conversation.

"Hey, thanks for taking me seriously."

"There's no need to thank me for your intuition." He smirks and gets up to leave the room.

A couple of minutes later, the clubhouse door opens, and I hear the sound of Trevor's voice.

Violet says, "She's in there."

Trevor opens the door and interrupts my privacy, causing me to sub-consciously tense and stand up.

"What do you want?" I scoff.

"I just wanted to say . . . I'm sorry. I had no reason for my actions. I was just . . . I was just angry, and Nate made it worse. But I am truly sorry for making you upset. I was kinda being an ass. I still want to be the boy you love."

"Thank you, Trevor. I forgive you. But the more you continue to act like this, the more I don't want to be with you."

"Thank you for forgiving me. I better go pick up dinner. I'm getting Joey's tonight—your favorite."

I smile weakly at him as he heads back into the hall.

Just before leaving, he glances at the "bathroom" door, and says, "Oh yeah. I gotta put the toilet in there soon."

The comment is so random and throws me off guard I don't say anything.

Although he apologized, something still doesn't feel the same as it did five months ago.

Something is missing.

"I'm back!" Trevor exclaims as he strides down the hall and over to the kitchen table, where we're sitting. Everyone returned to the clubhouse for dinner. Trevor sets the boxes on the table, revealing the mouth-watering smell of fresh, delicious pizza.

"Oh my god, it smells so good!" Teresa says.

"You got me pineapple and jalapeno, right?" Carla asks.

"And my pepperoni with extra cheese?" Nala adds.

"Yes, I got everything y'all asked for."

"Thank you, Trevor," Violet says.

"No biggie."

Trevor gives each of us our slices of pizza. With mine, he also hands me a milkshake.

"What is this?" I question.

"A strawberry milkshake with a cherry on top. My treat." Then he whispers more quietly, "You know, to make up for earlier."

"Wow, thanks! You're the best!"

The milkshake still doesn't change the feeling inside me. Something has changed in our relationship since August.

After dinner, Teresa pulls me outside to talk.

"So I guess you two made up now? You were pretty angry after what happened earlier."

"Yeah, I guess we did," I say with hesitation.

"What does that mean?"

"Well, he apologized earlier, and I forgave him. But something just isn't the same. I feel like . . . I don't know. I feel like something is missing."

"Well, that's a question you have to ask yourself."

I look at her with confusion, then understanding her tone, I continue. "I do still love him. I do. I mean, why wouldn't I? I don't know. I want to know what I really think, but it's like . . . my brain is locked."

"I can't tell you what you're thinking, but what I do know is you can't force yourself to be in a relationship you don't wanna be in. That's what I had to tell myself before I broke up with Josh."

The door swings open, and Trevor appears. "You guys coming, or what? We're about to start UNO."

"Okay, we're coming in second," I say.

He shuts the door behind us. I look back at Teresa. "Thank you for talking to me. I really needed this conversation."

"Anytime. If you ever need someone to talk to about relationship drama . . . or anything, you know who to come to. I'm always here for you."

"Thank you so much. Literally, you're such a good friend!"

CHAPTER 31
EMPTY HALLS, DANGER CALLS

Today is a new day. Raymond, Daniel, and Sadie's locations are still unknown. It's been more than a month since their gruesome—but apparently not so gruesome—attack at The Outlets. You'd think with this terrible hate group living in our town, more people would be talking about it. Nate and I get some glaring looks at school, but not as much as we should for the amount of times we're mentioned on the local news. Maybe it's a good thing to not have that recognition. I just wish more people would be worried about Raymond and Daniel, understanding they're actually a threat. But if their names are ever thrown around, everyone acts like it's a funny conspiracy theory.

I have an itching feeling that wherever Raymond, Daniel, and Sadie are and whatever they're doing, it won't be good for us. I keep telling my friends this, but they aren't listening. The only person listening to me is Nate. He knows I'm right, but he's afraid to say it because of how Trevor reacted last time. He knows the fear I'm feeling, and he understands because he's in the same position. The good thing is that Nate and I have a plan in case an emergency strikes.

I'm in the clubhouse "bathroom", combing my dark, greasy hair with Violet's brush. The door to the sleeping room is open, so I notice Nate the moment he enters.

His reflection wobbles in the small rectangular mirror Teresa stole from her mom's old vanity set.

"Hey. What's up?"

"Do you have a minute?" he asks.

"Yeah. What is it?"

He pulls a small red box out from his jean pocket. It's tied perfectly in a white bow.

"What's this?"

"Open it."

I untie the ribbon and carefully open the box to find a gorgeous silver necklace inside. I hold it in my hand and rub the deep blue charm with my thumb. The color is so mesmerizing, I can't stop staring at it. It's not just a simple blue, but I notice a tinge of green, maybe silver with it.

"Isn't that color nice? It reminds me of the pond back at the barn. That's why I picked it."

"Oh yes, it does! This color is so beautiful. But how were you able to buy it?"

"I used some of the money Violet gave me at Christmas."

"Are you serious?"

"Yeah," he says with a smile.

I feel my cheeks growing warm. I try to stop the blushing, but I can't. Nate squeezes his arm around me, and I put mine around his to complete the awkward but sweet half hug. He could have spent that money on himself, but the fact that he used it for me makes me feel special. What also makes it more special is that he didn't just buy the necklace to buy a necklace. He picked out a specific color that reminded him of a place we've spent many memorable days together.

"Thank you, Nate," I say, my mouth finally forming words. "This means a lot to me."

"Well . . . I'm glad you like it."

He walks out of the room. My fingers trace the lovely necklace as I clip it around my neck. I'm smiling and daydreaming about Nate when, all of a sudden, Trevor catches me off guard.

"Oh. Trevor . . ."

He's awkwardly gazing at my necklace.

"What do you want?"

He quickly switches his focus to my eyes.

"I have something for you."

Now I'm receiving a gift from two guys in one day. How pleasant.

He hands me a tiny bag with pink tissue paper. I tear away the paper to find another necklace, but with a cheap red heart charm.

"Wow, Trevor. It's . . . pretty. Thanks."

"Yep. Picked it out myself."

Please leave, Trevor, my brain is saying.

"Well, I need to finish in here, so . . ."

"Yeah. Right. I guess I'll just wait with everyone else. Anyway, happy Valentine's Day."

I completely forgot Valentine's Day existed. Now that explains all these gifts. The second he leaves the room, I mutter to myself, "Oh my god."

Which necklace am I supposed to wear now? after a minute of contemplation, I decide to stick with Nate's because it's prettier and has more meaning to it.

I take a deep breath and try my best to look confident as I walk outside to meet up with the rest of my friends. It's cold, but I've grown quite used to frigid temperatures after my time at the barn.

"Hey, Cal! Everything good?" Violet greets.

"Yeah, everything's fine."

"Did you not like my gift?" Trevor asks me in a hushed tone.

"No, I liked it. This one just matches my outfit more."

We start walking out of the woods and toward school. I slow my pace so I can walk with Teresa in the back. Nala is currently enthralled in a conversation with her. I do my best to divert Teresa's attention. Thankfully, it doesn't take long for her to notice.

"I think that's a great idea!" Teresa replies to Nala. Then she adds, "I'm sorry, can you give me and Cal a minute? I promise I'll be right back to finishing our conversation."

"Oh sure, that's totally chill."

Teresa steps away and asks, "Is everything all right?"

"It's fine. Just some annoying boy drama I don't want to get caught up in. I'm not trying to create a scene. It's just aggravating."

"I get it. Do you wanna tell me what happened?"

"Yeah, so Nate came in and gave me this necklace, the one I'm wearing now. Then Trevor came in a minute later and gave me another necklace, but the charm was different. Everything got really awkward. I don't want to hurt anyone's feelings. I just feel like crap."

"I can't believe they both got the same necklace. This literally feels like a Hallmark movie."

"Except that Hallmark movies are so predictable. This . . . not so much."

"Good point." Teresa laughs.

"I wish I wouldn't get so emotionally tied up by this. You know what I mean? My whole life doesn't revolve around boys, and I never asked for it to. I feel like me whining to you makes it seem like I'm upset only because of a boy . . . or two."

"I understand what you're saying. I don't feel like you're doing that. I feel like you're just stressed and annoyed because you don't need all this dumb drama interrupting your life."

"Oh my god, yes!"

I'm walking down the hall with Carla, Nala, Teresa, and Nate. We are on our way to the library to meet up with Violet and Trevor. We stay there for a little bit after school. Although we're able to walk or bike back to the clubhouse as soon as the last bell rings, we don't leave right away. It can get boring at the clubhouse, so this is a nice change in scenery.

The hallway is strangely empty today. I'm not sure why. I guess most of the students are toward the front of campus where the parking lot is. But with after-school activities and electives, there are normally students still roaming around at this time. "It feels weirdly quiet," I say. "Where is everyone?"

"I don't know. Maybe they're all in different classrooms or something," Teresa replies.

"Yeah, I guess. Something just feels off."

A moment later, we hear footsteps behind us and turn around to see Sadie. She's dressed in a gray tank top, black ripped jeans, black combat boots, and silver chain bracelets. Her outfit is a completely different style from the Sadie I once knew.

"What are you doing here?" I ask.

Carla, Teresa, and Nate huddle close to me, fearful and defensive. Nala stands a little more to the side, glaring at Sadie.

"I just wanted to drop by and say happy Valentine's Day to my bestie."

"You're a coward," Teresa scowls.

"You're really gonna call me a coward? I think you guys are the real cowards here. Especially you, Cal. I offered you the life of a billionaire and you decided to turn it down."

"We'd never fall for any of your stupid tricks," Nate says, gritting his teeth.

"I think you just did."

"What is she talking about?" Carla whispers in my ear. "What is she going to do this time?"

"I don't know. Just stay by me. We'll figure this out together."

"Carla, what's wrong?" Sadie mocks in a pouting voice. "Are you scared of me? How precious."

"Don't you dare mock my friends!" Nala defends. "You're just jealous you have none."

"C'mon guys. Let's just leave. This is stupid," Teresa says and we begin to walk away, but Raymond and Daniel enter through the other hallway and charge after us. They're both wearing black business suits. Is that the only outfit they have? Not the best choice for running around and fighting if you ask me.

"Long time no see . . . Calypso," Daniel hisses. "You know you got that name from us? You were originally Project Coalipo, but Stephanie and Dave decided they wanted a more . . . normalized name for you."

As if that's supposed to offend me. Sadie strides over to us while we attempt to run and grabs Nate and me by the wrists with her surprisingly strong grip. It's obvious she's gotten some fight training over the past few months.

"Remember the plan," I whisper to Nate, and he nods. Nate and I were right all along. Trevor should've listened to us instead of being so stubborn.

Raymond, with the help of Daniel, starts tying Carla and Teresa up to each other, back-to-back, while Sadie leads Nate and me toward the back exit. I keep waiting for at least one person to enter the hallway. Where is everyone? Raymond and Daniel must have done something so the other students wouldn't find us.

I watch in pain as Nala bolts toward Raymond and Daniel, about to attack, but is hurled to the floor with a bang. Teresa's muffled wails barely make it through the duct tape on her mouth. Carla begins to cry, but her bawling is also covered by duct tape. Daniel's foot on Nala's back is keeping them trapped. The three of them kick desperately for freedom.

Sadie is about to open the door when I yank my arms out of her grasp. I throw my fist at her and kick her in the gut. After a few more hits, Sadie is lying in pain against the cold white tiles. You don't know how long I've been wanting to do that. I'm not exactly sure where my sudden strength came from. I just took all my anger out on her, each hit harder than the last. To be honest, I surprised myself.

Raymond angrily sprints toward us while muttering under his breath. Daniel's foot digs more and more into Nala's back as they groan in agony. Nate whizzes in and out of a classroom to our left, and out of nowhere a blue chair flies across the hall and lands directly on top of Raymond.

"You evil kids!" Daniel shrieks. "What is wrong with you? I'm gonna make y'all regret you ever—"

Nate hands me another blue chair, and I interrupt Daniel by running over and slamming his whole body against the ground with it. Nala screams as he falls on top of them.

After Raymond and Daniel are knocked out, I look back to see Sadie motionless on the floor. I know she's awake. I didn't hit her that hard. She must've given up on fighting today, now that she's seen what happened to her leaders.

"Help . . . us," Nala gasps with the little breathing room they have left. I'm surprised they can still breathe at all with the weight of Daniel's body crushing them. Nate pushes Daniel away and releases Nala. I bite the thick brown rope with my teeth and loosen it until Carla and Teresa are free.

The reason I didn't use my powers against Raymond, Daniel, and Sadie is because then the whole world would pause, and I'd be alone with Nate. At some point I'd need to snap a second time so everything could unfreeze. If that had happened, Nala, Teresa, and Carla might have suffered more. This way the Deal and Do leaders are knocked out for a while, and we can find a teacher or another adult who can help us.

"Oh my god, that was brutal," Teresa says after tearing the duct tape off her mouth.

"You looked like a superhero!" Carla exclaims, her voice still shaking.

"Which one?" Nala asks.

"I don't think that matters right now."

Teresa steps to the side to comfort Nala and help them stand up.

"Really, I'm okay. Everything's gonna be okay," Nala says.

"I know, but you can barely walk." Teresa lifts the back of her shirt. "I know Daniel was—oh my god! Oh my god, that bruise."

"It's okay. It doesn't hurt that bad."

Nate and Carla run over to stand by Teresa's side.

"Holy shit. Yeah, he dug his shoe in real good," Nate adds. "There's marks from it. And that big bruise in the middle doesn't look good."

Nala chuckles. Their coping mechanism. But as more words spill out of their mouth, they begin to choke. "I'm telling you . . . I'll be fine."

Teresa's eyes begin to water. Carla wraps an arm around Teresa as she cries into her shoulder. I stand there, chewing my cheek and watching all this happen. I feel like I'm not really here. As if I'm looking at life through a screen. No, stop. You're strong. You need to lead. You need to support your friends. I suck in the nerves and guilt with a big deep breath.

"C'mon guys. We need to go before they wake back up."

"Yeah, we need to find the principal or someone," Nate says.

Teresa and Nate help Nala as they limp in laughing pain across the hall. Carla runs up to me. "We need to call an ambulance for them."

"Yep. I know. If we go to authorities and tell them, they'll call 911."

"What's wrong?" Carla questions, sensing my bitter tone.

"Nothing. I—I don't know. I feel like I failed."

"Don't say that. You didn't fail."

"I mean, look at you guys. Nala can barely walk, you and Teresa have chafe marks on your body from the duct tape and rope. Teresa is crying. And I'm the one that got y'all into this mess in the first place."

"None of that was in your control. I don't think you failed. You saved us. The fact Nala is able to walk at all is a miracle all because you and Nate planned for this. You know the life of survival."

"I mean yeah, I guess I do. after all those months in the barn—"

"Exactly. So stop telling yourself you're a bad leader. I aspire to have your confidence."

What confidence? Carla has all the confidence in the world. She is so carefree and doesn't worry about what anyone thinks of her. But who knows, maybe that's just how I perceive her.

"Where the hell is everyone anyway?" Nala asks.

"I don't know. That's what I was asking earlier."

We begin to wander through the halls, searching for someone. Anyone. We continue back to the cafeteria. after another minute or two, I hear voices. Familiar voices. Trevor and Violet. I run in that direction, the rest of my friends struggling behind me, their injuries still raw.

"Oh my god, we were looking everywhere for you guys."

"So were we," Trevor says.

"What happened?" Violet asks.

"Raymond and Daniel and Sadie . . . they all showed up."

"They were tying me and Teresa up and hurting us," Carla says. "Nala's back might be broken now. And Sadie was about to take Nate and Cal with her. It was so scary."

"Yeah, it wasn't pleasant," Nala says. "Daniel got this huge cut and bruise on my back. Probably gonna turn into a nasty scar."

"That's horrible! Do you need to go to the hospital?" Violet asks.

"I don't know. I probably broke something. I'll be fine though."

"We need to call 911. Where are they now?"

"Cal and Nate knocked them out with chairs!" Carla exclaims.

"What?" Trevor questions, flustered by all this news.

Not all of them. Sadie is still back there. Although she didn't seem determined to get revenge, she could appear behind our backs at any minute. We need to get out of here.

"Yeah, see? I was right after all," Nate says, glaring at Trevor. Trevor glares back.

Nate scoffs and rolls his eyes.

"Y'all, stop. We don't want another fight," I say.

"We would've come sooner," Violet explains, "but the principal said there was a hard lockdown and that we all needed to stay in the cafeteria. Apparently they heard of some bad news going on in the halls."

"Well, they weren't wrong," Teresa says.

"I bet Raymond and Daniel did something so the principal would do that, make everyone stay in one place."

Nate nods, agreeing with me.

"Can we talk about this later?" Teresa asks. "We need to go tell someone what happened before Raymond and Daniel wake up again and escape."

"Yeah, I know. Let's go," I declare, and the seven of us rush with the strength we have left to the front office.

CHAPTER 32
THE END?

R ed and blue lights flash behind me as Raymond and Daniel make their way to the police cars in handcuffs. I'm standing at the front of the school next to Nate and Trevor. Violet is standing with a police woman, immersed in conversation. Carla and Teresa are saying goodbye to Nala as they get loaded onto an ambulance. All the other students left a while ago. I feel relieved. No more running, no more hiding, no more fighting.

I catch a glimpse of Sadie out of the corner of my eye. I escape the crowd quietly and walk over to her. She looks at me as if I'm supposed to help. Part of me feels bad. She is only fifteen, and now she has to go to juvie. I am waiting for the police to run over here and handcuff her, but they're having Violet sign papers. I'm guessing property or guardian forms since I can't live with Violet's parents anymore. When the police arrived, we found Stephanie and Dave hiding in one of the science classrooms. They're arrested now too.

"You expect me to help you after all you've done to us?" I ask Sadie.

"Come with me. We could make a great team together."

"Why? So you can run away? I'm not becoming a criminal and making stupid decisions like you did. And how can I trust that you'll keep me alive? I bet you're lying to my face right now."

"You ran away before."

"That was because I was in danger, not because I fell for one of your stupid bullshit lies."

She stares me down with that manipulating look of hers and keeps quiet.

"It isn't too late to do the right thing, you know?"

"And I believe I am." She turns around and darts into the trees, out of sight.

I freeze up, not even processing what just happened. I feel angry because she ran away, sad because I lost a friend, confused because my life is full of shit I can't explain, but also confident because I'm stronger than I thought I was. I feel a tap on my shoulder and glance behind me to see Violet.

"What's wrong? Aren't you happy that Daniel and Raymond are finally arrested? And guess what? I'm now officially your guardian! Well, I technically haven't filled out all the paperwork yet, but still. Isn't that exciting?"

"That is." I try to smile, but I can't.

"What's troubling you?"

"Sadie . . . she ran away."

"What? When?"

"Just a second ago."

"Wait, for real? I didn't see her."

I look down at my shoes. Torn and dirty.

"What did she say?"

I laugh wryly. "She wanted me to come with her. I said no the second she asked. How stupid is she?"

"I don't know."

I grimace and look up at my sister, who is also now my guardian. My parent? No, that's too weird.

"I'm just so confused. I feel like all stories end with a happy and resolved ending and everything is perfect. I'm waiting for everything to feel perfect . . . but it doesn't."

"Your story isn't over yet, so of course, you're still going to have struggles, but each thing that happens in your life, good or bad, impacts who you are. It's all a part of your story, and your story is a part of who you are now and who you will become. But your story doesn't end until you do."

"Wow. I never thought about it that way," I admit.

Violet's words fill me with reassurance and hope, which urges me to return to the rest of my friends.

"You good?" Nate asks.

"Yeah, I'm great!"

Truth is, I feel better now but not great. I thought the police would help us. I thought they would handcuff Sadie right away, but they ignored her and let her run.

They didn't even notice.

Violet speaks up. "Did the police leave?"

"Yeah, they're going to continue searching for Sadie and keep us updated," Trevor informs.

So they did notice Sadie running away. But I still feel like they aren't taking us seriously. At least Raymond and Daniel are arrested, but now with Sadie on the loose, who knows what's to come? I sigh, and we grab our backpacks.

"Let's head to my house for dinner," Carla says. "I think my mom is making chicken pot pie casserole."

"Oh, that sounds lovely!" Violet exclaims.

"I'm so hungry . . . and tired," Teresa says.

"Me too."

And we all head off into the sunset together.

CHAPTER 33
A DREADFUL WEIGHT

Three months have passed since Raymond, Daniel, Stephanie, and Dave were arrested and Sadie ran away. I confronted the police multiple times to see if they had any more news on her whereabouts. Every time I called or went into the office, they shrugged it off, saying they're trying their hardest to make sure we stay safe, but there's nothing they can do right now. "It's all out of our hands," according to Lieutenant Robert Kramer, the officer leading this case. It angers me greatly that something affecting my entire everyday life means nothing to others.

The only thing I know is Sadie can definitely tell she's being watched. She's moving from one place to the next at the speed of a hare. Kramer mentioned the one consistent factor in Sadie's known locations is they're all out West. She was in Vegas at some point, and last I heard, I think she was in California. But the police aren't making any moves to actually catch her. Sadie has robbed two banks and stolen quite a hefty supply of Raymond and Daniel's weapons. Wherever she is, I don't want to confront her because I know danger will arise. Even if the police don't agree. "We're doing the best we can, sweetheart" is what Kramer says every time. It's sickening how much he belittles me.

After the main members of the Deal and Do were arrested, the other team partners grew fearful without their leaders to protect them. They all left the company. I have a feeling that definitely won't boost the leaders' reputations when they find out. They're going to want more members, and they're going to want them sooner rather than later. At least they're currently behind bars, so there's nothing they can do.

I should feel relieved. The Deal and Do Company has dissipated. The only members left are trapped in prison. Except Sadie. But she's one person. I shouldn't be worried. I should be enjoying the last few days of school before summer starts. Summer used to be my favorite season. I always looked forward to late night golf rides with friends, eating watermelon popsicles on hot days, shopping at The Outlets with friends, going to the pool, and basking in the sun. No longer is my life happy and normal.

The only feeling inside me right now is fear and dread. I'm dreading the future, what is to come. Sadie may be a lone ranger, but she is a loose cannon. And the leaders might be behind bars, but I'm beginning to think it won't be much longer until I see them again. Plus, my friends are growing weak. Nala had to stay in bed for a month and a half before their two broken ribs healed. What if we aren't strong enough to handle the events ahead? I won't feel relieved until I know I am far away from the Deal and Do. Until I know they are gone for good and that they won't return to make my life miserable. My enemies are still out there, and I have an aching gut feeling that when they return, they aren't going to hold anything back. Life is about to go downhill.

To be continued . . .

ACKNOWLEDGMENTS

I could not have published this book without all the people who helped me throughout the process. Just the fact that I began this series in middle school is an unbelievable statement, and I am overwhelmed with excitement thinking about everyone who will be reading my work.

My first thank you goes to my mom for being my biggest supporter. She let me read my drafts to her before they were even good. She believes in me when I'm feeling down and pushes me to never give up. I could not have done this without her. I'm also overly grateful for my mentor, Mrs. Hyland, who has been reading my drafts since day one. Many of our conversations sparked ideas that make the story what it is today.

I didn't begin this series with publishing in mind. As I was drafting the third book, I realized I wanted to get this story out into the world. But even then, I had no idea how to do this. I started giving up on the series entirely. In the fall of 2022, my film coach, Justin Sterner, read snippets of the book and asked thought-provoking questions that prompted me to quicken my pace and actually figure out my next steps. The following weekend, my mom ran into children's author Katie Lester, who introduced us to Mascot Books Publishing. After talking with her, I contacted the publishing group and now I'm here. Big shoutout to Justin, Katie, and the incredible team at Mascot/Amplify Publishing Group—Naren Aryal, Jess Cohn, Lauren Magnussen, Debbie Nosil, Nina Spahn, Gillian Barth, and Cypriene Madison.

My good friend, Maggie, deserves a special shoutout. She is so hardworking and never fails to amaze me with her artwork, as well as her editing and photography skills. Thank you so much, Maggie, for designing my cover art. The details are stunning and I loved working with you on this.

I have been blessed with so many other amazing friends and supporters as well. Spencer, Erin, Kaydence, Will, Ally, Zhuni, Conor, Zakk, Alexa, Emily M., Minu, and Natalie H., thank you for being such great friends and encouraging my ambitious endeavors. Thank you to everyone else in my film academy class at school who has shown their loving enthusiasm about this series, as well as my small group at church. It makes me so happy to see others looking forward to this project that I've put so much time and thought into. I'd also like to thank my older sister, Emma, for everything she has done for me, supporting my writing goals, and doing her best to stay strong even when life gets hard.

Lastly, I'd like to thank my sixth grade ELA teacher, Mrs. Wilhite, who led me to my love and passion for writing; my old friend, Avery, who helped me brainstorm during the early stages of this book; and my ninth grade English Lit teacher, Mrs. Brumbelow, for helping me strengthen my writing style and voice as an author.

I'm sure there are others who I am forgetting at the time, so thanks to everyone who contributed to this novel in some way, even if your name is not mentioned here. It's because of all these lovely people that the book is in your hands right now.

ABOUT THE AUTHOR

ISABELLA GERBORG is a teen author who lives near Atlanta, Georgia and is part of the film academy at her local high school. She is an aspiring screenwriter and director, and she hopes to continue working on drama and thriller stories in the future. Isabella was inspired to begin this series at thirteen years old as a way to escape into her imagination and fight boredom during the COVID-19 lockdown. When she's not writing or brainstorming, Isabella enjoys listening to music, hanging out with friends, and snuggling with her goldendoodle, Snickers. Isabella hopes to encourage other teens to find their passion and work hard to achieve what makes them happy, even if they aren't exactly sure what that is yet.